PENGUIN POPULAR CLASSICS

TWELFTH NIGHT
BY WILLIAM SHAKESPEARE

D0610846

PENGUIN POPULAR CLASSICS

TWELFTH NIGHT, OR, WHAT YOU WILL

WILLIAM SHAKESPEARE

PENGUIN BOOKS

PENGUIN BOOKS

Published by the Penguin Group
Penguin Books Ltd, 27 Wrights Lane, London w8 5tz, England
Penguin Putnam Inc., 375 Hudson Street, New York, New York 10014, USA
Penguin Books Australia Ltd, Ringwood, Victoria, Australia
Penguin Books Canada Ltd, 10 Alcorn Avenue, Toronto, Ontario, Canada m4v 3b2
Penguin Books (NZ) Ltd, Private Bag 102902, NSMC, Auckland, New Zealand

Penguin Books Ltd, Registered Offices: Harmondsworth, Middlesex, England

Published in Penguin Popular Classics 1994
9

CONTENTS

THE WORKS OF SHAKESPEARE

WILLIAM SHAKESPEARE

William Shakespeare was born at Stratford upon Avon in April, 1564. He was the third child, and eldest son, of John Shakespeare and Mary Arden. His father was one of the most prosperous men of Stratford who held in turn the chief offices in the town. His mother was of gentle birth, the daughter of Robert Arden of Wilmcote. In December, 1582, Shakespeare married Ann Hathaway, daughter of a farmer of Shottery, near Stratford; their first child Susanna was baptized on May 6, 1583, and twins, Hamnet and Judith, on February 22, 1585. Little is known of Shakespeare's early life; but it is unlikely that a writer who dramatized such an incomparable range and variety of human kinds and experiences should have spent his early manhood entirely in placid pursuits in a country town. There is one tradition, not universally accepted, that he fled from Stratford because he was in trouble for deer stealing, and had fallen foul of Sir Thomas Lucy, the local magnate; another that he was for some time a schoolmaster.

From 1592 onwards the records are much fuller. In March, 1592, the Lord Strange's players produced a new play at the Rose Theatre called *Harry the Sixth,* which was very successful, and was probably the *First Part of Henry VI.* In the autumn of 1592 Robert Greene, the best known of the professional writers, as he was dying wrote a letter to three fellow writers in which he warned them against the ingratitude of players in general, and in particular against an 'upstart crow' who 'supposes he is as much able to bombast out a blank verse as the best of you: and being an absolute Johannes Factotum is in his own conceit the only

Shake-scene in a country.' This is the first reference to Shakespeare, and the whole passage suggests that Shakespeare had become suddenly famous as a playwright. At this time Shakespeare was brought into touch with Edward Alleyne the great tragedian, and Christopher Marlowe, whose thundering parts of Tamburlaine, the Jew of Malta and Dr Faustus Alleyne was acting, as well as Hieronimo, the hero of Kyd's *Spanish Tragedy,* the most famous of all Elizabethan plays.

In April, 1593, Shakespeare published his poem *Venus and Adonis,* which was dedicated to the young Earl of Southampton : it was a great and lasting success, and was reprinted nine times in the next few years. In May, 1594, his second poem, *The Rape of Lucrece,* was also dedicated to Southampton.

There was little playing in 1593, for the theatres were shut during a severe outbreak of the plague; but in the autumn of 1594, when the plague ceased, the playing companies were re-organized, and Shakespeare became a sharer in the Lord Chamberlain's company who went to play in the Theatre in Shoreditch. During these months Marlowe and Kyd had died. Shakespeare was thus for a time without a rival. He had already written the three parts of *Henry VI,* *Richard III, Titus Andronicus, Two Gentlemen of Verona,* *Love's Labour's Lost, The Comedy of Errors,* and *The Taming of the Shrew.* Soon afterwards he wrote the first of his greater plays – *Romeo and Juliet* – and he followed this success in the next three years with *A Midsummer Night's Dream, Richard II,* and *The Merchant of Venice.* The two parts of *Henry IV,* introducing Falstaff, the most popular of all his comic characters, were written in 1597–8.

The company left the Theatre in 1597 owing to disputes over a renewal of the ground lease, and went to play at the

Curtain in the same neighbourhood. The disputes contin-ued throughout 1598, and at Christmas the players settled the matter by demolishing the old Theatre and re-erecting a new playhouse on the South bank of the Thames, near Southwark Cathedral. This playhouse was named the Globe. The expenses of the new building were shared by the chief members of the Company, including Shakespeare, who was now a man of some means. In 1596 he had bought New Place, a large house in the centre of Stratford, for £60, and through his father purchased a coat-of-arms from the Heralds, which was the official recognition that he and his family were gentlefolk.

By the summer of 1598 Shakespeare was recognized as the greatest of English dramatists. Booksellers were print-ing his more popular plays, at times even in pirated or stolen versions, and he received a remarkable tribute from a young writer named Francis Meres, in his book *Palladis Tamia*. In a long catalogue of English authors Meres gave Shakespeare more prominence than any other writer, and mentioned by name twelve of his plays.

Shortly before the Globe was opened, Shakespeare had completed the cycle of plays dealing with the whole story of the Wars of the Roses with *Henry V*. It was followed by *As You Like it,* and *Julius Caesar,* the first of the maturer tragedies. In the next three years he wrote *Troylus and Cressida, The Merry Wives of Windsor, Hamlet,* and *Twelfth Night.*

On March 24, 1603, Queen Elizabeth died. The company had often performed before her, but they found her suc-cessor a far more enthusiastic patron. One of the first acts of King James was to take over the company and to pro-mote them to be his own servants so that henceforward they were known as the King's Men. They acted now very frequently at Court, and prospered accordingly. In the early years of the reign Shakespeare wrote the more sombre comedies, *All's Well that Ends Well*, and *Measure for Measure*, which were followed by *Othello, Macbeth* and *King Lear*. Then he returned to Roman themes with *Antony and Cleopatra* and *Coriolanus*.

Since 1601 Shakespeare had been writing less, and there were now a number of rival dramatists who were introducing new styles of drama, particularly Ben Jonson (whose first successful comedy, *Every Man in his Humour*, was acted by Shakespeare's company in 1598), Chapman, Dekker, Marston, and Beaumont and Fletcher who began to write in 1607. In 1608 the King's Men acquired a second playhouse, an indoor private-theatre in the fashionable quarter of the Blackfriars. At private theatres, plays were performed indoors; the prices charged were higher than in the public playhouses, and the audience consequently was more select. Shakespeare seems to have retired from the stage about this time: his name does not occur in the various lists of players after 1607. Henceforward he lived for the most part at Stratford where he was regarded as one of the most important citizens. He still wrote a few plays, and he tried his hand at the new form of tragi-comedy – a play with tragic incidents but a happy ending – which Beaumont and Fletcher had popularized. He wrote four of these – *Pericles, Cymbeline, The Winter's Tale* and *The Tempest*, which was acted at Court in 1611. For the last four years of his life he lived in retirement. His son Hamnet had died in 1596: his two daughters were now married. Shakespeare died in Stratford upon Avon on April 23, 1616, and was buried at the chancel of the church, before the high altar. Shortly afterwards a memorial which still exists, with a portrait bust, was set up on the North wall. His wife survived him.

When Shakespeare died fourteen of his plays had been separately published in Quarto booklets. In 1623 his surviving fellow actors, John Heming and Henry Condell, with the co-operation of a number of printers, published a collected edition of thirty-six plays in one Folio volume, with an engraved portrait, memorial verses by Ben Jonson and others, and an Epistle to the Reader in which Heming and Condell make the interesting note that Shakespeare's 'hand and mind went together, and what he thought, he uttered with that easiness that we have scarce received from him a blot in his papers.'

The plays as printed in the Quartos or the Folio differ considerably from the usual modern text. They are often not divided into scenes, and sometimes not even into acts. Nor are there place-headings at the beginning of each scene, because in the Elizabethan theatre there was no scenery. They are carelessly printed and the spelling is erratic.

THE ELIZABETHAN THEATRE

Although plays of one sort and another had been acted for many generations, no permanent playhouse was erected in England until 1576. In the 1570's the Lord Mayor and Aldermen of the City of London and the players were constantly at variance. As a result James Burbage, then the leader of the great Earl of Leicester's players, decided that he would erect a playhouse outside the jurisdiction of the Lord Mayor, where the players would no longer be hindered by the authorities. Accordingly in 1576 he built the Theatre in Shoreditch, at that time a suburb of London. The experiment was successful, and by 1592 there were two more playhouses in London, the Curtain (also in Shore-ditch), and the Rose on the south bank of the river, near Southwark Cathedral.

Elizabethan players were accustomed to act on a variety of stages; in the great hall of a nobleman's house, or one of the Queen's palaces, in town halls and in yards, as well as their own theatre.

The public playhouse for which most of Shakespeare's plays were written was a small and intimate affair. The outside measurement of the Fortune Theatre, which was built in 1600 to rival the new Globe, was but eighty feet square. Playhouses were usually circular or octagonal, with three tiers of galleries looking down upon the yard or pit, which was open to the sky. The stage jutted out into the yard so that the actors came forward into the midst of their audience.

Over the stage there was a roof, and on either side doors by which the characters entered or disappeared. Over the back of the stage ran a gallery or upper stage which was used whenever an upper scene was needed, as when Romeo climbs up to Juliet's bedroom, or the citizens of Angiers address King John from the walls. The space beneath this upper stage was known as the tiring house; it was concealed from the audience by a curtain which could be drawn back to reveal an inner stage, for such scenes as the witches' cave in Macbeth, Prospero's cell, or Juliet's tomb.

There was no general curtain concealing the whole stage, so that all scenes on the main stage began with an entrance and ended with an exit. Thus in tragedies the dead must be carried away. There was no scenery, and therefore no limit to the number of scenes, for a scene came to an end when the characters left the stage. When it was necessary for the exact locality of a scene to be known, then Shakespeare

THE GLOBE THEATRE

Wood-engraving by R. J. Beedham after a reconstruction by J. C. Adams

indicated it in the dialogue; otherwise a simple property or a garment was sufficient; a chair or stool showed an indoor scene, a man wearing riding boots was a messenger, a king wearing armour was on the battlefield, or the like. Such simplicity was on the whole an advantage; the spectator was not distracted by the setting and Shakespeare was able to use as many scenes as he wished. The action passed by very quickly; a play of 2500 lines of verse could be acted in two hours. Moreover since the actor was so close to his audience, the slightest subtlety of voice and gesture was easily appreciated.

The company was a 'Fellowship of Players', who were all partners and sharers. There were usually ten to fifteen full members, with three or four boys, and some paid servants. Shakespeare had therefore to write for his team. The chief actor in the company was Richard Burbage, who first distinguished himself as Richard III; for him Shakespeare wrote his great tragic parts. An important member of the company was the clown or low comedian. From 1594 to 1600 the company's clown was Will Kemp; he was succeeded by Robert Armin. No women were allowed to appear on the stage, and all women's parts were taken by boys.

*

TWELFTH NIGHT

The earliest mention of *Twelfth Night* occurs in the diary of John Manningham, a barrister of the Middle Temple, which is now in the British Museum. Under the date 2nd February, 1602 he noted:

'At our feast we had a play called "Twelfth Night, or What you Will," much like the Comedy of Errors, or Menechmi in Plautus, but most like and near to that in Italian called *Inganni*. A good practice in it to make the Steward believe his Lady widow was in love with him, by counterfeiting a letter as from his Lady in general terms, telling him what she liked best in him, and prescribing his gesture in smiling, his apparel, etc., and then when he came to practise making him believe they took him to be mad.'

The hall of the Middle Temple, where the play was acted, remained intact until 1940 when it was badly damaged in an air raid.

The play was then fairly new, as can be seen from the several references to current events in the dialogue, which are more frequent than usual in Shakespeare's plays. Thus Maria's simile of Malvolio smiling 'his face into more lines than is in the new map with the augmentation of the Indies' (p. 69) is a reminiscence of the notable map of the world published in 1600; and Fabian's remark about a 'pension of thousands to be paid from the Sophy' was apt in the late months of 1601 when a popular account of the adventures of Sir Anthony Shirley and his company at the Court of the Shah of Persia was first published. These and other topicalities are more fully set out in the notes.

The main plot of the play Shakespeare apparently took from the tale of *Apolonius and Silla*, which was one of the stories in Barnabe Riche's *Farewell to the Military Profession*, though similar tales are not uncommon. The story of Apolonius and Silla runs thus:

Once upon a time there was a Duke called Pontus, who was governor of the isle of Cyprus. He had two children, very much alike, Silvio, a son, and Silla, a daughter. It chanced that Apolonius, the young Duke of Constantinople, visited Cyprus on his way back from an expedition against the Turks. Silla fell in love with Apolonius, and when he had gone, she determined to follow him. She persuaded her servant, Pedro, to go with her and to pretend that she was his sister. Whilst they were at sea, the captain of the vessel began to woo her and then to threaten her, but a storm arose, and the ship was wrecked, Silla alone being brought to shore on the captain's sea chest. Being thus cast away alone on a foreign shore, Silla bethought her of the dangers threatening an unprotected maid. She therefore disguised herself in the captain's clothes, and pretended to be a man, taking the name of her brother. Then she went to the Court of Apolonius, and as 'Silvio' became his servant, and was soon high in his favour.

Now Apolonius was wooing a wealthy widow named Julina, and 'Silvio' was constantly sent as his messenger to the lady. Soon Julina fell in love with the pretty courtier and declared her passion. About this time the real Silvio appeared in Constantinople. He had guessed where Silla had gone and was searching for her. As he walked the streets of Constantinople Julina met him, and mistaking him for the disguised Silla, she called him by name and invited him to her house. Silvio was not a little surprised, but accepted the invitation and spent the night alone with Julina. Next morning, when he pondered the adventure, he knew there must be some mistake and thought it more discreet to continue his journey. Meanwhile Duke Apolonius became importunate. Julina replied that she was now married. Hereupon the Duke's servants told him how intimate his 'Silvio' had become with the widow, with the result that Silla found herself in a dungeon. Julina soon realized that she was with child. She went to the Duke to claim 'Silvio.' Silvio was therefore called before them and denied all connection with Julina so vehemently that both she and the Duke began to grow angry. Things were now in such a tangle that Silla could no longer conceal her sex. She took Julina aside and revealed her secret. Apolonius was so greatly astonished at Silla's love and devotion that he married her. Meanwhile the report of these events reached the real Silvio, who hurried back to Constantinople and married Julina. So they all lived happily ever afterwards.

It is noticeable that in using this story, or its like, for his play Shakespeare somewhat altered the emphasis. The theme of *Apolonius and Silla* is that a maid in love will go to any lengths to win her man, but in *Twelfth Night* the stress is laid rather on the love of sister for brother, genuine as Viola's for Sebastian, sentimental as Olivia's for her brother's memory. It may be merely coincidence that a few months before the play was written there had been a very remarkable case of the love of a sister for her brother in high life. Margaret Ratcliffe, one of the Queen's Maids of Honour, was notoriously devoted to her brother, Sir Alexander Ratcliffe. He was killed in Ireland in the summer of 1599. Hearing the news she pined away and died of a broken heart six months later. She was buried in Westminster Abbey and her pathetic death was much talked of.

The gulling of the puritan Malvolio, especially where his

tormentors pretend that he is possessed, owes something to the sensational case of the exorcist, John Darrell, who had cast devils out of various afflicted Puritans. The ecclesiastical authorities, believing Darrell to be a fraud, imprisoned him, and an official pamphlet exposing his fraudulent practices was printed in 1599. Darrell, however, had many friends, who published pamphlets in his defence. From one of these, *A Discourse concerning the certain possession and dispossession of seven persons in one family in Lancashire*, written by Darrell's colleague, George More, Shakespeare took a few phrases and ideas, notably the famous yellow stockings.

The drunken party which led up to Malvolio's troubles was also very similar to an event which was argued at length in the Court of the Star Chamber in the winter of 1601. Some years before Sir Thomas Posthumus Hoby, who was a silly little man with an overpowering mother, married a Lady Sidney, who had in her own right considerable property in Yorkshire. The Yorkshire squires did not approve of Sir Thomas, who was fussy and puritanical. One afternoon in August, 1600, a party of them who had been hunting came to his house and invited themselves for the night.

'Sir Thomas, who had previously sent word that they would not be welcome, sat grudgingly with his guests at supper, when they entertained each other in discourses of horses and dogs (sports unto which Sir Thomas never applied himself), partly in lascivious talk and great oaths, partly in inordinate drinking of healths (an abuse never practised by Sir Thomas). After supper Sir Thomas had their chambers made ready, and came to conduct them thither himself, but they answered that they would finish their game of dice first. Hoby descended to the hall to family prayers, and when the strains of a psalm mounted upwards, the revellers began to stamp with their feet and to make other rude noises. Next morning at breakfast, when they called for more wine, Sir Thomas sent for the key of the cellar to prevent it. They then fell again to play, and shortly after, one of his servants came out and told them peremptorily that their play was offensive to Lady Hoby and willed them to depart the house. Hoby, meanwhile, had shut himself in the study. The leader of the party therefore craved admittance to Lady Hoby, and took his leave. They then left the mansion with many noisy threats and much abuse, even calling its master a scurvy urchin and a spindle-shanked ape.

Sir Thomas petitioned the Council for redress, and after the usual passing to and fro of complaints and answers, the case came before the Star Chamber in January, 1602. There was good matter for a play in this story.'

[For further accounts of this and the other events to which Shakespeare refers in *Twelfth Night,* and for the original authorities, see my *Second* and *Last Elizabethan Journals,* and *Shakespeare at Work,* pp. 283–297.]

Twelfth Night was not published until the first Folio of 1623. The text is well printed, with few misprints or unintelligible readings. There are signs that in parts a revision was made to suit a change in the caste. In Act One, Scene Two, Viola declared her intention of serving the Duke as a singer, but the songs are sung by the Clown. It has been suggested that originally the boy who took the part of Viola was a singer, but that at a later revival some slight alterations were made to enable the Clown to take the songs.

The present text is a compromise. It follows the Folio closely. Spelling is modernized, but the original arrangement and punctuation (which 'points' the text for reading aloud) have been left, except where they seemed definitely wrong. A few emendations generally accepted by editors have been kept. The reader who is used to an 'accepted text' may thus find certain unfamiliarities, but the text itself is nearer to that used in Shakespeare's own playhouse.

•

Twelfth Night,
or, What you Will

THE ACTORS' NAMES

ORSINO, Duke of Illyria
SEBASTIAN, brother to Viola
ANTONIO, a sea captain, friend to Sebastian
A Sea Captain, friend to Viola
VALENTINE ⎫
CURIO ⎭ gentlemen attending on the Duke
SIR TOBY BELCH, uncle to Olivia
SIR ANDREW AGUECHEEK
MALVOLIO, steward to Olivia
FABIAN ⎫
FESTE, a Clown ⎭ servants to Olivia
OLIVIA
VIOLA
MARIA, Olivia's gentlewoman

*

Enter Orsino, Duke of Illyria, Curio, and other Lords.

DUKE: If music be the food of Love, play on,
  Give me excess of it: that surfeiting,
  The appetite may sicken, and so die.
  That strain again, it had a dying fall:
  O, it came o'er my ear, like the sweet sound
  That breathes upon a bank of violets;
  Stealing, and giving odour. Enough, no more,
  'Tis not so sweet now, as it was before.
  O spirit of Love, how quick and fresh art thou,
  That notwithstanding thy capacity,
  Receiveth as the sea, nought enters there,
  Of what validity, and pitch soe'er,
  But falls into abatement, and low price
  Even in a minute; so full of shapes is fancy,
  That it alone, is high fantastical.

CURIO: Will you go hunt my Lord?

DUKE: What Curio?

CURIO: The hart.

DUKE: Why so I do, the noblest that I have:
  O when mine eyes did see Olivia first,
  Methought she purg'd the air of pestilence;
  That instant was I turn'd into a hart,
  And my desires like fell and cruel hounds,
  E'er since pursue me. How now what news from her?

Enter Valentine.

VALENTINE: So please my Lord, I might not be admitted,
  But from her handmaid do return this answer:
  The Element itself, till seven years' heat,

Shall not behold her face at ample view:
But like a cloistress she will veiled walk,
And water once a day her chamber round
With eye-offending brine: all this to season
A brother's dead love, which she would keep fresh
And lasting, in her sad remembrance.

DUKE: O she that hath a heart of that fine frame
To pay this debt of love but to a brother,
How will she love, when the rich golden shaft
Hath kill'd the flock of all affections else
That live in her. When liver, brain, and heart,
These sovereign thrones, are all suppli'd, and fill'd
Her sweet perfections with one self king:
Away before me, to sweet beds of flowers,
Love-thoughts lie rich, when canopi'd with bowers.
                                 Exeunt.

I. 2

Enter Viola, a Captain, and Sailors.

VIOLA: What country, friends, is this?

CAPTAIN: This is Illyria Lady.

VIOLA: And what should I do in Illyria?
My brother he is in Elysium,
Perchance he is not drown'd: what think you sailors?

CAPTAIN: It is perchance that you yourself were saved.

VIOLA: O my poor brother, and so perchance may he be.

CAPTAIN: True Madam, and to comfort you with chance,
Assure yourself, after our ship did split,
When you, and those poor number saved with you,
Hung on our driving boat: I saw your brother
Most provident in peril, bind himself,
(Courage and hope both teaching him the practice)

To a strong mast, that liv'd upon the sea:
Where like Orion on the dolphin's back,
I saw him hold acquaintance with the waves,
So long as I could see.

VIOLA: For saying so, there's gold:
Mine own escape unfoldeth to my hope,
Whereto thy speech serves for authority
The like of him. Know'st thou this country?

CAPTAIN: Ay Madam well, for I was bred and born
Not three hours' travel from this very place.

VIOLA: Who governs here?

CAPTAIN: A noble Duke in nature, as in name.

VIOLA: What is his name?

CAPTAIN: Orsino.

VIOLA: Orsino: I have heard my father name him.
He was a bachelor then.

CAPTAIN: And so is now, or was so very late:
For but a month ago I went from hence,
And then 'twas fresh in murmur (as you know
What great ones do, the less will prattle of)
That he did seek the love of fair Olivia.

VIOLA: What's she?

CAPTAIN: A virtuous maid, the daughter of a Count
That died some twelvemonth since, then leaving her
In the protection of his son, her brother,
Who shortly also died: for whose dear love
(They say) she hath abjur'd the sight
And company of men.

VIOLA: O that I serv'd that Lady,
And might not be delivered to the world
Till I had made mine own occasion mellow
What my estate is.

CAPTAIN: That were hard to compass,

Because she will admit no kind of suit,
No, not the Duke's.

VIOLA: There is a fair behaviour in thee Captain,
And though that nature, with a beauteous wall
Doth oft close in pollution: yet of thee
I will believe thou hast a mind that suits
With this thy fair and outward character.
I prithee (and I'll pay thee bounteously)
Conceal me what I am, and be my aid,
For such disguise as haply shall become
The form of my intent. I'll serve this Duke,
Thou shalt present me as an eunuch to him,
It may be worth thy pains: for I can sing,
And speak to him in many sorts of music,
That will allow me very worth his service.
What else may hap, to time I will commit,
Only shape thou thy silence to my wit.

CAPTAIN: Be you his eunuch, and your mute I'll be,
When my tongue blabs, then let mine eyes not see.

VIOLA: I thank thee: lead me on.

Exeunt.

I. 3

Enter Sir Toby, and Maria.

SIR TOBY: What a plague means my niece to take the death
of her brother thus? I am sure care's an enemy to life.

MARIA: By my troth Sir Toby, you must come in earlier
a' nights: your cousin, my Lady, takes great exceptions
to your ill hours.

SIR TOBY: Why let her except, before excepted.

MARIA: Ay, but you must confine yourself within the
modest limits of order.

SIR TOBY: Confine? I'll confine myself no finer than I am: these clothes are good enough to drink in, and so be these boots too: and they be not, let them hang themselves in their own straps.

MARIA: That quaffing and drinking will undo you: I heard my Lady talk of it yesterday: and of a foolish knight that you brought in one night here, to be her wooer.

SIR TOBY: Who, Sir Andrew Ague-cheek?

MARIA: Ay he.

SIR TOBY: He's as tall a man as any's in Illyria.

MARIA: What's that to th' purpose?

SIR TOBY: Why he has three thousand ducats a year.

MARIA: Ay, but he'll have but a year in all these ducats: he's a very fool, and a prodigal.

SIR TOBY: Fie, that you'll say so: he plays o' th' viol-de-gamboys, and speaks three or four languages word for word without book, and hath all the good gifts of nature.

MARIA: He hath indeed, almost natural: for besides that he's a fool, he's a great quarreller: and but that he hath the gift of a coward, to allay the gust he hath in quarrelling, 'tis thought among the prudent, he would quickly have the gift of a grave.

SIR TOBY: By this hand they are scoundrels and substractors that say so of him. Who are they?

MARIA: They that add moreover, he's drunk nightly in your company.

SIR TOBY: With drinking healths to my niece: I'll drink to her as long as there is a passage in my throat, and drink in Illyria: he's a coward and a coystrill that will not drink to my niece till his brains turn o' th' toe, like a parish-top. What wench? Castiliano vulgo: for here comes Sir Andrew Agueface.

Enter Sir Andrew.

SIR ANDREW: Sir Toby Belch. How now Sir Toby Belch?

SIR TOBY: Sweet Sir Andrew.

SIR ANDREW: Bless you fair shrew.

MARIA: And you too sir.

SIR TOBY: Accost Sir Andrew, accost.

SIR ANDREW: What's that?

SIR TOBY: My niece's chambermaid.

SIR ANDREW: Good Mistress Accost, I desire better acquaintance.

MARIA: My name is Mary sir.

SIR ANDREW: Good Mistress Mary Accost.

SIR TOBY: You mistake knight: accost, is front her, board her, woo her, assail her.

SIR ANDREW: By my troth I would not undertake her in this company. Is that the meaning of accost?

MARIA: Fare you well gentlemen.

SIR TOBY: And thou let part so Sir Andrew, would thou mightst never draw sword again.

SIR ANDREW: And you part so mistress, I would I might never draw sword again: fair lady, do you think you have fools in hand?

MARIA: Sir, I have not you by th' hand.

SIR ANDREW: Marry but you shall have, and here's my hand.

MARIA: Now sir, thought is free: I pray you bring your hand to th' buttery-bar, and let it drink.

SIR ANDREW: Wherefore, sweet-heart? What's your metaphor?

MARIA: It's dry sir.

SIR ANDREW: Why I think so; I am not such an ass, but I can keep my hand dry. But what's your jest?

MARIA: A dry jest sir.

SIR ANDREW: Are you full of them?

MARIA: Ay sir, I have them at my fingers' ends: marry now I let go your hand, I am barren.

Exit Maria.

SIR TOBY: O knight, thou lack'st a cup of Canary: when did I see thee so put down?

SIR ANDREW: Never in your life I think, unless you see Canary put me down: methinks sometimes I have no more wit than a Christian, or an ordinary man has: but I am a great eater of beef, and I believe that does harm to my wit.

SIR TOBY: No question.

SIR ANDREW: And I thought that, I'd forswear it. I'll ride home to-morrow Sir Toby.

SIR TOBY: *Pourquoi* my dear knight?

SIR ANDREW: What is *pourquoi*? Do, or not do? I would I had bestowed that time in the tongues, that I have in fencing, dancing and bear-baiting: O had I but followed the Arts.

SIR TOBY: Then hadst thou had an excellent head of hair.

SIR ANDREW: Why, would that have mended my hair?

SIR TOBY: Past question, for thou seest it will not cool my nature.

SIR ANDREW: But it becomes me well enough, does't not?

SIR TOBY: Excellent, it hangs like flax on a distaff; and I hope to see a housewife take thee between her legs, and spin it off.

SIR ANDREW: Faith I'll home to-morrow Sir Toby, your niece will not be seen, or if she be it's four to one, she'll none of me: the Count himself here hard by, woos her.

SIR TOBY: She'll none o' th' Count, she'll not match above her degree, neither in estate, years, nor wit: I have heard her swear 't. Tut there's life in 't man.

SIR ANDREW: I'll stay a month longer. I am a fellow o' th' strangest mind i' th' world; I delight in Masques and Revels sometimes altogether.

SIR TOBY: Art thou good at these kickchawses, knight?

SIR ANDREW: As any man in Illyria, whatsoever he be, under the degree of my betters, and yet I will not compare with an old man.

SIR TOBY: What is thy excellence in a galliard, knight?

SIR ANDREW: Faith, I can cut a caper.

SIR TOBY: And I can cut the mutton to 't.

SIR ANDREW: And I think I have the back-trick, simply as strong as any man in Illyria.

SIR TOBY: Wherefore are these things hid? Wherefore have these gifts a curtain before 'em? Are they like to take dust, like Mistress Mall's picture? Why dost thou not go to church in a galliard, and come home in a coranto? My very walk should be a jig: I would not so much as make water but in a sink-a-pace: what dost thou mean? Is it a world to hide virtues in? I did think by the excellent constitution of thy leg, it was form'd under the star of a galliard.

SIR ANDREW: Ay, 'tis strong, and it does indifferent well in a damn'd-colour'd stock. Shall we sit about some Revels?

SIR TOBY: What shall we do else: were we not born under Taurus?

SIR ANDREW: Taurus? That's sides and heart.

SIR TOBY: No sir, it is legs and thighs: let me see thee caper. Ha, higher: ha, ha, excellent.

Exeunt.

Enter Valentine, and Viola in man's attire.

VALENTINE: If the Duke continue these favours towards you Cesario, you are like to be much advanc'd, he hath known you but three days, and already you are no stranger.

VIOLA: You either fear his humour, or my negligence, that you call in question the continuance of his love. Is he inconstant sir, in his favours?

VALENTINE: No believe me.

Enter Duke, Curio, and Attendants.

VIOLA: I thank you: here comes the Count.

DUKE: Who saw Cesario hoa?

VIOLA: On your attendance my Lord here.

DUKE: Stand you a while aloof. Cesario,
Thou know'st no less, but all: I have unclasp'd
To thee the book even of my secret soul.
Therefore good youth, address thy gait unto her,
Be not deni'd access, stand at her doors,
And tell them, there thy fixed foot shall grow
Till thou have audience.

VIOLA: Sure my noble Lord,
If she be so abandon'd to her sorrow
As it is spoke, she never will admit me.

DUKE: Be clamorous, and leap all civil bounds,
Rather than make unprofited return.

VIOLA: Say I do speak with her (my Lord) what then?

DUKE: O then, unfold the passion of my love,
Surprise her with discourse of my dear faith;
It shall become thee well to act my woes:
She will attend it better in thy youth,
Than in a nuntio's of more grave aspect.

VIOLA: I think not so, my Lord.
DUKE: Dear lad, believe it;
  For they shall yet belie thy happy years,
  That say thou art a man: Diana's lip
  Is not more smooth, and rubious: thy small pipe
  Is as the maiden's organ, shrill, and sound,
  And all is semblative a woman's part.
  I know thy constellation is right apt
  For this affair: some four or five attend him,
  All if you will: for I myself am best
  When least in company: prosper well in this,
  And thou shalt live as freely as thy Lord,
  To call his fortunes thine.
VIOLA: I'll do my best
  To woo your Lady: yet a barful strife,
  Whoe'er I woo, myself would be his wife.

Exeunt.

I.5

Enter Maria, and Clown.

MARIA: Nay, either tell me where thou hast been, or I
  will not open my lips so wide as a bristle may enter, in
  way of thy excuse: my Lady will hang thee for thy
  absence.
CLOWN: Let her hang me: he that is well hang'd in this
  world, needs to fear no colours.
MARIA: Make that good.
CLOWN: He shall see none to fear.
MARIA: A good lenten answer: I can tell thee where that
  saying was born, of I fear no colours.
CLOWN: Where good Mistress Mary?

MARIA: In the wars, and that may you be bold to say in your foolery.

CLOWN: Well, God give them wisdom that have it: and those that are fools, let them use their talents.

MARIA: Yet you will be hang'd for being so long absent, or to be turn'd away: is not that as good as a hanging to you?

CLOWN: Many a good hanging, prevents a bad marriage: and for turning away, let summer bear it out.

MARIA: You are resolute then?

CLOWN: Not so neither, but I am resolv'd on two points.

MARIA: That if one break, the other will hold: or if both break, your gaskins fall.

CLOWN: Apt in good faith, very apt: well go thy way, if Sir Toby would leave drinking, thou wert as witty a piece of Eve's flesh, as any in Illyria.

MARIA: Peace you rogue, no more o' that: here comes my Lady. make your excuse wisely, you were best.

Exit.

Enter Lady Olivia, with Malvolio.

CLOWN: Wit, and't be thy will, put me into good fooling: those wits that think they have thee, do very oft prove fools: and I that am sure I lack thee, may pass for a wise man. For what says Quinapalus, Better a witty fool, than a foolish wit.   God bless thee Lady.

OLIVIA: Take the fool away.

CLOWN: Do you not hear fellows, take away the Lady.

OLIVIA: Go to, y'are a dry fool: I'll no more of you: besides you grow dishonest.

CLOWN: Two faults Madonna, that drink and good counsel will amend: for give the dry fool drink, then is the fool not dry: bid the dishonest man mend himself, if he mend, he is no longer dishonest; if he cannot, let the botcher mend him: anything that's mended, is but patch'd: virtue that transgresses, is but patch'd with sin, and sin that amends, is but patch'd with virtue. If that this simple syllogism will serve, so: if it will not, what remedy? As there is no true cuckold but calamity, so beauty's a flower; the Lady bade take away the fool, therefore I say again, take her away.

OLIVIA: Sir, I bade them take away you.

CLOWN: Misprision in the highest degree. Lady, *Cucullus non facit monachum*: that's as much to say, as I wear not motley in my brain: good Madonna, give me leave to prove you a fool.

OLIVIA: Can you do it?

CLOWN: Dexteriously, good Madonna.

OLIVIA: Make your proof.

CLOWN: I must catechize you for it Madonna. Good my Mouse of virtue answer me.

OLIVIA: Well sir, for want of other idleness, I'll bide your proof.

CLOWN: Good Madonna, why mourn'st thou?

OLIVIA: Good fool, for my brother's death.

CLOWN: I think his soul is in hell, Madonna.

OLIVIA: I know his soul is in heaven, fool.

CLOWN: The more fool, Madonna, to mourn for your brother's soul, being in heaven. Take away the fool, gentlemen.

OLIVIA: What think you of this fool Malvolio, doth he not mend?

MALVOLIO: Yes, and shall do, till the pangs of death shake him: infirmity that decays the wise, doth ever make the better fool.

CLOWN: God send you sir, a speedy infirmity, for the

better increasing your folly: Sir Toby will be sworn
that I am no fox, but he will not pass his word for two
pence that you are no fool.

OLIVIA: How say you to that Malvolio?

MALVOLIO: I marvel your Ladyship takes delight in such
a barren rascal: I saw him put down the other day, with
an ordinary fool, that has no more brain than a stone.
Look you now, he's out of his guard already: unless you
laugh and minister occasion to him, he is gagg'd. I protest
I take these wise men, that crow so at these set kind of
fools, no better than the fools' zanies.

OLIVIA: O you are sick of self-love Malvolio, and taste
with a distemper'd appetite. To be generous, guiltless,
and of free disposition, is to take those things for bird-
bolts, that you deem cannon-bullets: there is no slander
in an allow'd fool, though he do nothing but rail; nor no
railing, in a known discreet man, though he do nothing
but reprove.

CLOWN: Now Mercury indue thee with leasing, for thou
speak'st well of fools.

Enter Maria.

MARIA: Madam, there is at the gate, a young gentleman,
much desires to speak with you.

OLIVIA: From the Count Orsino, is it?

MARIA: I know not, Madam, 'tis a fair young man, and
well attended.

OLIVIA: Who of my people hold him in delay?

MARIA: Sir Toby Madam, your kinsman.

OLIVIA: Fetch him off I pray you, he speaks nothing but
madman: fie on him. [*Exit Maria.*] Go you Malvolio; if
it be a suit from the Count, I am sick, or not at home.
What you will, to dismiss it. [*Exit Malvolio.*] Now you
see sir, how your fooling grows old, and people dislike it.

CLOWN: Thou hast spoke for us, Madonna, as if thy eldest
son should be a fool: whose skull, Jove cram with brains,
for here he comes.

Enter Sir Toby.

One of thy kin has a most weak *pia mater.*

OLIVIA: By mine honour half drunk. What is he at the
gate cousin?

SIR TOBY: A gentleman.

OLIVIA: A gentleman? What gentleman?

SIR TOBY: 'Tis a gentleman here. A plague o' these pickle-
herring: how now sot.

CLOWN: Good Sir Toby.

OLIVIA: Cousin, cousin, how have you come so early by
this lethargy?

SIR TOBY: Lechery, I defy lechery: there's one at the gate.

OLIVIA: Ay marry, what is he?

SIR TOBY: Let him be the devil and he will, I care not: give
me faith say I. Well, it's all one.

Exit.

OLIVIA: What's a drunken man like, fool?

CLOWN: Like a drown'd man, a fool, and a mad man: one
draught above heat, makes him a fool, the second mads
him, and the third drowns him.

OLIVIA: Go thou and seek the crowner, and let him sit o'
my coz; for he's in the third degree of drink: he's
drown'd: go look after him.

CLOWN: He is but mad yet Madonna, and the fool shall
look to the madman.

Exit.

Enter Malvolio.

MALVOLIO: Madam, yond young fellow swears he will
speak with you. I told him you were sick, he takes on
him to understand so much, and therefore comes to speak

with you. I told him you were asleep, he seems to have a foreknowledge of that too, and therefore comes to speak with you. What is to be said to him Lady, he's fortified against any denial?

OLIVIA: Tell him, he shall not speak with me.

MALVOLIO: Has been told so: and he says he'll stand at your door like a Sheriff's post, and be the supporter to a bench, but he'll speak with you.

OLIVIA: What kind o' man is he?

MALVOLIO: Why of mankind.

OLIVIA: What manner of man?

MALVOLIO: Of very ill manner: he'll speak with you, will you, or no.

OLIVIA: Of what personage, and years is he?

MALVOLIO: Not yet old enough for a man, nor young enough for a boy: as a squash is before 'tis a peascod, or a codling when 'tis almost an apple: 'tis with him in standing water, between boy and man. He is very well-favour'd, and he speaks very shrewishly: one would think his mother's milk were scarce out of him:

OLIVIA: Let him approach: call in my gentlewoman.

MALVOLIO: Gentlewoman, my Lady calls.
Exit.
Enter Maria.

OLIVIA: Give me my veil: come throw it o'er my face,
We'll once more hear Orsino's embassy.
Enter Viola.

VIOLA: The honourable Lady of the house, which is she?

OLIVIA: Speak to me, I shall answer for her: your will?

VIOLA: Most radiant, exquisite, and unmatchable beauty. I pray you tell me if this be the Lady of the house, for I never saw her. I would be loath to cast away my speech: for besides that it is excellently well penn'd, I have taken great pains to con it. Good beauties, let me sustain no scorn; I am very comptible, even to the least sinister usage.

OLIVIA: Whence came you sir?

VIOLA: I can say little more than I have studied, and that question's out of my part. Good gentle one, give me modest assurance, if you be the Lady of the house, that I may proceed in my speech.

OLIVIA: Are you a comedian?

VIOLA: No my profound heart: and yet (by the very fangs of malice, I swear) I am not that I play. Are you the Lady of the house?

OLIVIA: If I do not usurp myself, I am.

VIOLA: Most certain, if you are she, you do usurp yourself: for what is yours to bestow, is not yours to reserve. But this is from my commission: I will on with my speech in your praise, and then show you the heart of my message.

OLIVIA: Come to what is important in't: I forgive you the praise.

VIOLA: Alas, I took great pains to study it, and 'tis poetical.

OLIVIA: It is the more like to be feigned, I pray you keep it in. I heard you were saucy at my gates, and allow'd your approach rather to wonder at you, than to hear you. If you be not mad, be gone: if you have reason, be brief: 'tis not that time of moon with me, to make one in so skipping a dialogue.

MARIA: Will you hoist sail sir, here lies your way.

VIOLA: No good swabber, I am to hull here a little longer. Some mollification for your giant, sweet Lady; tell me your mind, I am a messenger.

OLIVIA: Sure you have some hideous matter to deliver, when the courtesy of it is so fearful. Speak your office.

VIOLA: It alone concerns your ear: I bring no overture of war, no taxation of homage; I hold the olive in my hand: my words are as full of peace, as matter.

OLIVIA: Yet you began rudely. What are you? What would you?

VIOLA: The rudeness that hath appear'd in me, have I learn'd from my entertainment. What I am, and what I would, are as secret as maiden-head: to your ears, divinity; to any other's, profanation.

OLIVIA: Give us the place alone, we will hear this divinity.

Exit Maria.

Now sir, what is your text?

VIOLA: Most sweet Lady.

OLIVIA: A comfortable doctrine and much may be said of it. Where lies your text?

VIOLA: In Orsino's bosom.

OLIVIA: In his bosom? In what chapter of his bosom?

VIOLA: To answer by the method, in the first of his heart.

OLIVIA: O, I have read it: it is heresy. Have you no more to say?

VIOLA: Good Madam, let me see your face.

OLIVIA: Have you any commission from your Lord, to negotiate with my face: you are now out of your text: but we will draw the curtain, and show you the picture. Look you sir, such a one I was this present: is't not well done?

VIOLA: Excellently done, if God did all.

OLIVIA: 'Tis in grain sir, 'twill endure wind and weather.

VIOLA: 'Tis beauty truly blent, whose red and white,
Nature's own sweet, and cunning hand laid on:
Lady, you are the cruell'st she alive,
If you will lead these graces to the grave,
And leave the world no copy.

OLIVIA: O sir, I will not be so hard-hearted: I will give out
divers schedules of my beauty. It shall be inventoried and
every particle and utensil labell'd to my will: as, Item
two lips indifferent red: Item two grey eyes, with lids to
them: Item, one neck, one chin, and so forth. Were you
sent hither to praise me?

VIOLA: I see you what you are, you are too proud:
But if you were the devil, you are fair:
My Lord and master loves you: O such love
Could be but recompens'd, though you were crown'd
The nonpareil of beauty.

OLIVIA: How does he love me?

VIOLA: With adorations, fertile tears,
With groans that thunder love, with sighs of fire.

OLIVIA: Your Lord does know my mind, I cannot love
him:
Yet I suppose him virtuous, know him noble,
Of great estate, of fresh and stainless youth;
In voices well divulg'd, free, learn'd, and valiant,
And in dimension, and the shape of nature,
A gracious person; but yet I cannot love him:
He might have took his answer long ago.

VIOLA: If I did love you in my master's flame,
With such a suffering, such a deadly life:
In your denial, I would find no sense,
I would not understand it.

OLIVIA: Why, what would you?

VIOLA: Make me a willow cabin at your gate,
And call upon my soul within the house,
Write loyal cantons of contemned love,
And sing them loud even in the dead of night:
Hallo your name to the reverberate hills,
And make the babbling gossip of the air,

Cry out Olivia: O you should not rest
Between the elements of air, and earth,
But you should pity me.
OLIVIA: You might do much:
  What is your parentage?
VIOLA: Above my fortunes, yet my state is well:
  I am a gentleman.
OLIVIA: Get you to your Lord:
  I cannot love him: let him send no more,
  Unless (perchance) you come to me again,
  To tell me how he takes it: fare you well:
  I thank you for your pains: spend this for me.
VIOLA: I am no fee'd post, Lady; keep your purse,
  My master, not myself, lacks recompense.
  Love make his heart of flint, that you shall love,
  And let your fervour like my master's be,
  Plac'd in contempt: farewell fair cruelty.
                    Exit.
OLIVIA: What is your parentage?
  Above my fortunes, yet my state is well;
  I am a gentleman. I'll be sworn thou art;
  Thy tongue, thy face, thy limbs, actions, and spirit,
  Do give thee five-fold blazon: not too fast: soft, soft,
  Unless the master were the man. How now?
  Even so quickly may one catch the plague?
  Methinks I feel this youth's perfections
  With an invisible, and subtle stealth
  To creep in at mine eyes. Well, let it be.
  What hoa, Malvolio.
                Enter Malvolio.
MALVOLIO: Here Madam, at your service.
OLIVIA: Run after that same peevish messenger
  The County's man: he left this ring behind him

Would I, or not: tell him, I'll none of it.
Desire him not to flatter with his Lord,
Nor hold him up with hopes, I am not for him:
If that the youth will come this way to-morrow,
I'll give him reasons for't: hie thee Malvolio.

MALVOLIO: Madam, I will.

Exit.

OLIVIA: I do I know not what, and fear to find
Mine eye too great a flatterer for my mind:
Fate, show thy force, ourselves we do not owe,
What is decreed, must be: and be this so.

Exit.

II. 1

Enter Antonio and Sebastian.

ANTONIO: Will you stay no longer: nor will you not that
I go with you?

SEBASTIAN: By your patience, no: my stars shine darkly
over me; the malignancy of my fate, might perhaps
distemper yours; therefore I shall crave of you your
leave, that I may bear my evils alone. It were a bad recompense for your love, to lay any of them on you.

ANTONIO: Let me yet know of you, whither you are
bound.

SEBASTIAN: No sooth sir: my determinate voyage is mere
extravagancy. But I perceive in you so excellent a touch
of modesty, that you will not extort from me, what I am
willing to keep in: therefore it charges me in manners,
the rather to express myself: you must know of me then
Antonio, my name is Sebastian (which I call'd Roderigo)
my father was that Sebastian of Messaline, whom I know
you have heard of. He left behind him, myself, and a

sister, both born in an hour: if the Heavens had been
pleas'd, would we had so ended. But you sir, alter'd that,
for some hour before you took me from the breach of
the sea, was my sister drown'd.

ANTONIO: Alas the day.

SEBASTIAN: A Lady sir, though it was said she much re-
sembled me, was yet of many accounted beautiful: but
though I could not with such estimable wonder over-far
believe that, yet thus far I will boldly publish her, she
bore a mind that envy could not but call fair: she is
drown'd already sir with salt water, though I seem to
drown her remembrance again with more.

ANTONIO: Pardon me sir, your bad entertainment.

SEBASTIAN: O good Antonio, forgive me your trouble.

ANTONIO: If you will not murther me for my love, let me
be your servant.

SEBASTIAN: If you will not undo what you have done,
that is kill him, whom you have recover'd, desire it not.
Fare ye well at once, my bosom is full of kindness, and I
am yet so near the manners of my mother, that upon the
least occasion more, mine eyes will tell tales of me: I am
bound to the Count Orsino's Court, farewell.

Exit.

ANTONIO: The gentleness of all the gods go with thee:
I have many enemies in Orsino's Court,
Else would I very shortly see thee there:
But come what may, I do adore thee so,
That danger shall seem sport, and I will go.

Exit.

Enter Viola and Malvolio, at several doors.

MALVOLIO: Were not you even now, with the Countess Olivia?

VIOLA: Even now sir, on a moderate pace, I have since arriv'd but hither.

MALVOLIO: She returns this ring to you (sir) you might have saved me my pains, to have taken it away yourself. She adds moreover, that you should put your Lord into a desperate assurance, she will none of him. And one thing more, that you be never so hardy to come again in his affairs, unless it be to report your Lord's taking of this: receive it so.

VIOLA: She took the ring of me, I'll none of it.

MALVOLIO: Come sir, you peevishly threw it to her: and her will is, it should be so return'd: if it be worth stooping for, there it lies, in your eye: if not, be it his that finds it.

Exit.

VIOLA: I left no ring with her: what means this Lady?
Fortune forbid my outside have not charm'd her:
She made good view of me, indeed so much,
That sure methought her eyes had lost her tongue,
For she did speak in starts distractedly.
She loves me sure, the cunning of her passion
Invites me in this churlish messenger:
None of my Lord's ring? Why he sent her none:
I am the man, if it be so, as 'tis,
Poor Lady, she were better love a dream:
Disguise, I see thou art a wickedness,
Wherein the pregnant enemy does much.

How easy is it, for the proper-false
In women's waxen hearts to set their forms:
Alas, our frailty is the cause, not we,
For such as we are made, if such we be:
How will this fadge? My master loves her dearly,
And I (poor monster) fond as much on him:
And she (mistaken) seems to dote on me:
What will become of this? As I am man,
My state is desperate for my master's love:
As I am woman (now alas the day)
What thriftless sighs shall poor Olivia breathe?
O time, thou must untangle this, not I,
It is too hard a knot for me t' untie.

Exit.

II. 3

Enter Sir Toby, and Sir Andrew.

SIR TOBY: Approach Sir Andrew: not to be a-bed after midnight, is to be up betimes, and *diluculo surgere*, thou know'st.

SIR ANDREW: Nay by my troth I know not: but I know, to be up late, is to be up late.

SIR TOBY: A false conclusion: I hate it as an unfill'd can. To be up after midnight, and to go to bed then is early: so that to go to bed after midnight, is to go to bed betimes. Does not our lives consist of the four elements?

SIR ANDREW: Faith so they say, but I think it rather consists of eating and drinking.

SIR TOBY: Th'art a scholar; let us therefore eat and drink. Marian I say, a stoup of wine.

Enter Clown.

SIR ANDREW: Here comes the fool i' faith.

CLOWN: How now my hearts: did you never see the picture of we three?

SIR TOBY: Welcome ass, now let's have a catch.

SIR ANDREW: By my troth the fool has an excellent breast. I had rather than forty shillings I had such a leg, and so sweet a breath to sing, as the fool has. In sooth thou wast in very gracious fooling last night, when thou spök'st of Pigrogromitus, of the Vapians passing the Equinoctial of Queubus: 'twas very good i' faith: I sent thee sixpence for thy leman, hadst it?

CLOWN: I did impeticos thy gratillity: for Malvolio's nose is no whipstock: my lady has a white hand, and the Myrmidons are no bottle-ale houses.

SIR ANDREW: Excellent: why this is the best fooling, when all is done. Now a song.

SIR TOBY: Come on, there is sixpence for you. Let's have a song.

SIR ANDREW: There's a testril of me too: if one knight give a—

CLOWN: Would you have a love-song, or a song of good life?

SIR TOBY: A love-song, a love-song.

SIR ANDREW: Ay, ay. I care not for good life.

CLOWN [sings]:

  O mistress mine where are you roaming?
  O stay and hear, your true love's coming,
    That can sing both high and low.
  Trip no further pretty sweeting;
  Iourneys end in lovers meeting,
    Every wise man's son doth know.

SIR ANDREW: Excellent good, i' faith.

SIR TOBY: Good, good.

CLOWN [sings]:

What is love, 'tis not hereafter,
Present mirth, hath present laughter:
  What's to come, is still unsure.
In delay there lies no plenty,
Then come kiss me sweet and twenty:
  Youth's a stuff will not endure.

SIR ANDREW: A mellifluous voice, as I am true knight.

SIR TOBY: A contagious breath.

SIR ANDREW: Very sweet, and contagious i' faith.

SIR TOBY: To hear by the nose, it is dulcet in contagion. But shall we make the welkin dance indeed? Shall we rouse the night-owl in a catch, that will draw three souls out of one weaver? Shall we do that?

SIR ANDREW: And you love me, let's do't: I am dog at a catch.

CLOWN: By'r lady sir, and some dogs will catch well.

SIR ANDREW: Most certain: let our catch be, *Thou knave.*

CLOWN: *Hold thy peace, thou knave* knight. I shall be constrain'd in't, to call thee knave, knight.

SIR ANDREW: 'Tis not the first time I have constrained one to call me knave. Begin fool: it begins, *Hold thy peace.*

CLOWN: I shall never begin if I hold my peace.

SIR ANDREW: Good i' faith: come begin.

Catch sung.
Enter Maria.

MARIA: What a caterwauling do you keep here? If my Lady have not call'd up her Steward Malvolio, and bid him turn you out of doors, never trust me.

SIR TOBY: My Lady's a Cataian, we are politicians, Malvolio's a Peg-a-Ramsey, and *Three merry men be we.* Am not I consanguineous? Am I not of her blood: tillyvally. Lady, *There dwelt a man in Babylon, Lady, Lady.*

CLOWN: Beshrew me, the knight's in admirable fooling.

SIR ANDREW: Ay, he does well enough if he be dispos'd, and so do I too: he does it with a better grace, but I do it more natural.

SIR TOBY: *O the twelfth day of December.*

MARIA: For the love o' God, peace.

Enter Malvolio.

MALVOLIO: My masters are you mad? Or what are you? Have you no wit, manners, nor honesty, but to gabble like tinkers at this time of night? Do ye make an alehouse of my Lady's house, that ye squeak out your coziers' catches without any mitigation or remorse of voice? Is there no respect of place, persons, nor time in you?

SIR TOBY: We did keep time sir in our catches. Sneck up.

MALVOLIO: Sir Toby, I must be round with you. My Lady bade me tell you, that though she harbours you as her kinsman, she's nothing alli'd to your disorders. If you can separate yourself and your misdemeanours, you are welcome to the house: if not, and it would please you to take leave of her, she is very willing to bid you farewell.

SIR TOBY: Farewell dear heart, since I must needs be gone.

MARIA: Nay good Sir Toby.

CLOWN: His eyes do show his days are almost done.

MALVOLIO: Is't even so?

SIR TOBY: But I will never die.

CLOWN: Sir Toby, there you lie.

MALVOLIO: This is much credit to you.

SIR TOBY: *Shall I bid him go?*

CLOWN: *What an if you do?*

SIR TOBY: *Shall I bid him go, and spare not?*

CLOWN: *O no, no, no, no, you dare not.*

SIR TOBY: Out o' tune sir, ye lie: art any more than a Steward? Dost thou think because thou art virtuous, there shall be no more cakes and ale?

CLOWN: Yes by Saint Anne, and ginger shall be hot i' th' mouth too.

SIR TOBY: Th'art i' th' right. Go sir, rub your chain with crums. A stoup of wine, Maria.

MALVOLIO: Mistress Mary, if you priz'd my Lady's favour at any thing more than contempt, you would not give means for this uncivil rule; she shall know of it by this hand.

Exit.

MARIA: Go shake your ears.

SIR ANDREW: 'Twere as good a deed as to drink when a man's a-hungry, to challenge him the field, and then to break promise with him, and make a fool of him.

SIR TOBY: Do't knight, I'll write thee a challenge: or I'll deliver thy indignation to him by word of mouth.

MARIA: Sweet Sir Toby be patient for to-night: since the youth of the Count's was to-day with my Lady, she is much out of quiet. For Monsieur Malvolio, let me alone with him: if I do not gull him into a nayword, and make him a common recreation, do not think I have wit enough to lie straight in my bed: I know I can do it.

SIR TOBY: Possess us, possess us, tell us something of him.

MARIA: Marry sir, sometimes he is a kind of Puritan.

SIR ANDREW: O, if I thought that, I'd beat him like a dog.

SIR TOBY: What for being a Puritan, thy exquisite reason, dear knight.

SIR ANDREW: I have no exquisite reason for't, but I have reason good enough.

MARIA: The devil a Puritan that he is, or any thing constantly but a time-pleaser, an affection'd ass, that cons state without book, and utters it by great swarths. The best persuaded of himself: so crammed (as he thinks) with excellencies, that it is his grounds of faith, that all that look on him, love him: and on that vice in him, will my revenge find notable cause to work.

SIR TOBY: What wilt thou do?

MARIA: I will drop in his way some obscure epistles of love, wherein by the colour of his beard, the shape of his leg, the manner of his gait, the expressure of his eye, forehead, and complexion, he shall find himself most feelingly personated. I can write very like my Lady your niece, on a forgotten matter we can hardly make distinction of our hands.

SIR TOBY: Excellent, I smell a device.

SIR ANDREW: I have't in my nose too.

SIR TOBY: He shall think by the letters that thou wilt drop that they come from my niece, and that she's in love with him.

MARIA: My purpose is indeed a horse of that colour.

SIR ANDREW: And your horse now would make him an ass.

MARIA: Ass, I doubt not.

SIR ANDREW: O 'twill be admirable.

MARIA: Sport royal I warrant you: I know my physic will work with him, I will plant you two, and let the fool make a third, where he shall find the letter: observe his construction of it: for this night to bed, and dream on the event: farewell.

Exit.

SIR TOBY: Good night Penthesilea.

SIR ANDREW: Before me she's a good wench.

SIR TOBY: She's a beagle true-bred, and one that adores me: what o' that?

SIR ANDREW: I was ador'd once too.

SIR TOBY: Let's to bed knight: thou hadst need send for more money.

SIR ANDREW: If I cannot recover your niece, I am a foul way out.

SIR TOBY: Send for money knight, if thou hast her not i' th' end, call me Cut.

SIR ANDREW: If I do not, never trust me, take it how you will.

SIR TOBY: Come, come, I'll go burn some sack, 'tis too late to go to bed now: come knight, come knight.

Exeunt.

II.4

Enter Duke, Viola, Curio, and others.

DUKE: Give me some music: now good morrow friends.
Now good Cesario, but that piece of song,
That old and antique song we heard last night;
Methought it did relieve my passion much,
More than light airs, and recollected terms
Of these most brisk and giddy-paced times.
Come, but one verse.

CURIO: He is not here (so please your Lordship) that should sing it.

DUKE: Who was it?

CURIO: Feste the jester my Lord, a fool that the Lady Olivia's father took much delight in. He is about the house.

DUKE: Seek him out, and play the tune the while.

Exit Curio. Music plays.

Come hither boy, if ever thou shalt love
In the sweet pangs of it, remember me;
For such as I am, all true lovers are,

Unstaid and skittish in all motions else,
Save in the constant image of the creature
That is belov'd. How dost thou like this tune?

VIOLA: It gives a very echo to the seat
Where Love is thron'd.

DUKE: Thou dost speak masterly,
My life upon 't, young though thou art, thine eye
Hath stay'd upon some favour that it loves:
Hath it not boy?

VIOLA: A little, by your favour.

DUKE: What kind of woman is't?

VIOLA: Of your complexion.

DUKE: She is not worth thee then. What years i' faith?

VIOLA: About your years my Lord.

DUKE: Too old by heaven: let still the woman take
An elder than herself, so wears she to him;
So sways she level in her husband's heart:
For boy, however we do praise ourselves,
Our fancies are more giddy and unfirm,
More longing, wavering, sooner lost and worn,
Than women's are.

VIOLA: I think it well my Lord.

DUKE: Then let thy love be younger than thyself,
Or thy affection cannot hold the bent:
For women are as roses, whose fair flower
Being once display'd, doth fall that very hour.

VIOLA: And so they are: alas, that they are so:
To die, even when they to perfection grow.

Enter Curio and Clown.

DUKE: O fellow come, the song we had last night:
Mark it Cesario, it is old and plain;
The spinsters and the knitters in the sun,
And the free maids that weave their thread with bones,

Do use to chant it: it is silly sooth,
And dallies with the innocence of love,
Like the old age.

CLOWN: Are you ready sir?

DUKE: Ay prithee sing.

Music.
The Song.

CLOWN: *Come away, come away death,*
   And in sad cypress let me be laid:
Fly away, fly away breath,
   I am slain by a fair cruel maid:
My shroud of white, stuck all with yew,
      O prepare it:
My part of death no one so true
      Did share it.

Not a flower, not a flower sweet,
   On my black coffin, let there be strown:
Not a friend, not a friend greet
   My poor corpse, where my bones shall be thrown:
A thousand thousand sighs to save,
      Lay me, O, where
Sad true lover never find my grave,
      To weep there.

DUKE: There's for thy pains.

CLOWN: No pains sir, I take pleasure in singing sir.

DUKE: I'll pay thy pleasure then.

CLOWN: Truly sir, and pleasure will be paid one time, or another.

DUKE: Give me now leave, to leave thee.

CLOWN: Now the melancholy god protect thee, and the tailor make thy doublet of changeable taffeta, for thy mind is a very opal. I would have men of such constancy

put to sea, that their business might be every thing, and
their intent every where, for that's it, that always makes
a good voyage of nothing. Farewell.

Exit.

DUKE: Let all the rest give place: once more Cesario,
   Get thee to yond same sovereign cruelty:
   Tell her my love, more noble than the world
   Prizes not quantity of dirty lands,
   The parts that Fortune hath bestow'd upon her:
   Tell her I hold as giddily as Fortune:
   But 'tis that miracle and Queen of Gems
   That nature pranks her in, attracts my soul.

VIOLA: But if she cannot love you sir?

DUKE: I cannot be so answer'd.

VIOLA: Sooth but you must.
   Say that some Lady, as perhaps there is,
   Hath for your love as great a pang of heart
   As you have for Olivia: you cannot love her:
   You tell her so: must she not then be answer'd?

DUKE: There is no woman's sides
   Can bide the beating of so strong a passion,
   As love doth give my heart: no woman's heart
   So big, to hold so much, they lack retention.
   Alas, their love may be call'd appetite,
   No motion of the liver, but the palate,
   That suffer surfeit, cloyment, and revolt,
   But mine is all as hungry as the sea,
   And can digest as much, make no compare
   Between that love a woman can bear me,
   And that I owe Olivia.

VIOLA: Ay but I know.

DUKE: What dost thou know?

VIOLA: Too well what love women to men may owe:

In faith they are as true of heart, as we.
My father had a daughter lov'd a man,
As it might be perhaps, were I a woman
I should your Lordship.

DUKE: And what's her history?

VIOLA: A blank my Lord: she never told her love,
But let concealment like a worm i' th' bud
Feed on her damask cheek: she pin'd in thought,
And with a green and yellow melancholy,
She sat like Patience on a Monument,
Smiling at grief. Was not this love indeed?
We men may say more, swear more, but indeed
Our shows are more than will: for still we prove
Much in our vows, but little in our love.

DUKE: But died thy sister of her love my boy?

VIOLA: I am all the daughters of my father's house,
And all the brothers too: and yet I know not.
Sir, shall I to this Lady?

DUKE: Ay that's the theme,
To her in haste: give her this jewel: say,
My love can give no place, bide no delay.

Exeunt.

II. 5

Enter Sir Toby, Sir Andrew, and Fabian.

SIR TOBY: Come thy ways Signior Fabian.

FABIAN: Nay I'll come: if I lose a scruple of this sport, let
me be boil'd to death with melancholy.

SIR TOBY: Wouldst thou not be glad to have the niggardly
rascally sheep-biter, come by some notable shame?

FABIAN: I would exult man: you know he brought me out
o' favour with my Lady, about a bear-baiting here.

SIR TOBY: To anger him we'll have the bear again, and we will fool him black and blue, shall we not Sir Andrew?

SIR ANDREW: And we do not, it is pity of our lives.

Enter Maria.

SIR TOBY: Here comes the little villain: how now my metal of India?

MARIA: Get ye all three into the box-tree: Malvolio's coming down this walk; he has been yonder i' the sun practising behaviour to his own shadow this half hour: observe him for the love of mockery: for I know this letter will make a contemplative idiot of him. Close in the name of jesting, lie thou there: for here comes the trout, that must be caught with tickling.

Exit.

Enter Malvolio.

MALVOLIO: 'Tis but Fortune, all is Fortune. Maria once told me she did affect me, and I have heard herself come thus near, that should she fancy, it should be one of my complexion. Besides she uses me with a more exalted respect, than any one else that follows her. What should I think on't?

SIR TOBY: Here's an overweening rogue.

FABIAN: Oh peace: contemplation makes a rare turkey-cock of him, how he jets under his advanc'd plumes.

SIR ANDREW: 'Slight I could so beat the rogue.

SIR TOBY: Peace I say.

MALVOLIO: To be Count Malvolio.

SIR TOBY: Ah rogue.

SIR ANDREW: Pistol him, pistol him.

SIR TOBY: Peace, peace.

MALVOLIO: There is example for't: the Lady of the Strachy, married the yeoman of the wardrobe.

SIR ANDREW: Fie on him Jezebel.

FABIAN: O peace, now he's deeply in: look how imagination blows him.

MALVOLIO: Having been three months married to her, sitting in my state.

SIR TOBY: O for a stone-bow to hit him in the eye.

MALVOLIO: Calling my officers about me, in my branch'd velvet gown: having come from a day-bed, where I have left Olivia sleeping.

SIR TOBY: Fire and brimstone.

FABIAN: O peace, peace.

MALVOLIO: And then to have the humour of state: and after a demure travel of regard: telling them I know my place, as I would they should do theirs: to ask for my kinsman Toby.

SIR TOBY: Bolts and shackles.

FABIAN: O peace, peace, peace, now, now.

MALVOLIO: Seven of my people with an obedient start, make out for him: I frown the while, and perchance wind up my watch, or play with my – some rich jewel: Toby approaches; courtesies there to me.

SIR TOBY: Shall this fellow live?

FABIAN: Though our silence be drawn from us with cars, yet peace.

MALVOLIO: I extend my hand to him thus: quenching my familiar smile with an austere regard of control.

SIR TOBY: And does not Toby take you a blow o' the lips, then?

MALVOLIO: Saying, Cousin Toby, my fortunes having cast me on your niece, give me this prerogative of speech.

SIR TOBY: What, what?

MALVOLIO: You must amend your drunkenness.

SIR TOBY: Out scab.

FABIAN: Nay patience, or we break the sinews of our plot.

MALVOLIO: Besides you waste the treasure of your time, with a foolish knight.

SIR ANDREW: That's me I warrant you.

MALVOLIO: One Sir Andrew.

SIR ANDREW: I knew 'twas I, for many do call me fool.

MALVOLIO: What employment have we here?

FABIAN: Now is the woodcock near the gin.

SIR TOBY: O peace, and the spirit of humours intimate reading aloud to him.

MALVOLIO: By my life this is my Lady's hand: these be her very *C's*, her *U's*, and her *T's*, and thus makes she her great *P's*. It is in contempt of question her hand.

SIR ANDREW: Her *C's*, her *U's*, and her *T's*: why that?

MALVOLIO: [*reads*] – *To the unknown belov'd this and my good wishes*: her very phrases: by your leave wax. Soft, and the impressure her Lucrece, with which she uses to seal: 'tis my Lady: to whom should this be?

FABIAN: This wins him, liver and all.

MALVOLIO: *Jove knows I love, but who. Lips do not move, no man must know*. No man must know. What follows? the numbers alter'd: no man must know, if this should be thee Malvolio?

SIR TOBY: Marry hang thee brock.

MALVOLIO: *I may command where I adore,*
 But silence like a Lucrece knife:
With bloodless stroke my heart doth gore,
 M.O.A.I. doth sway my life.

FABIAN: A fustian riddle.

SIR TOBY: Excellent wench, say I.

MALVOLIO: *M. O. A. I.* doth sway my life. Nay but first let me see, let me see, let me see.

FABIAN: What dish a' poison has she dressed him?

SIR TOBY: And with what wing the staniel checks at it?

MALVOLIO: *I may command, where I adore:* Why she may command me: I serve her, she is my Lady. Why this is evident to any formal capacity. There is no obstruction in this, and the end: what should that alphabetical position portend, if I could make that resemble something in me? Softly, *M. O. A. I.*

SIR TOBY: O ay, make up that, he is now at a cold scent.

FABIAN: Sowter will cry upon't for all this, though it be as rank as a fox.

MALVOLIO: *M.* Malvolio, *M.* why that begins my name.

FABIAN: Did not I say he would work it out, the cur is excellent at faults.

MALVOLIO: *M.* But then there is no consonancy in the sequel, that suffers under probation: *A* should follow, but *O* does.

FABIAN: And *O* shall end, I hope.

SIR TOBY: Ay, or I'll cudgel him, and make him cry *O.*

MALVOLIO: And then *I* comes behind.

FABIAN: Ay, and you had any eye behind you, you might see more detraction at your heels, than fortunes before you.

MALVOLIO: *M, O, A, I.* This simulation is not as the former: and yet to crush this a little, it would bow to me, for every one of these letters are in my name. Soft, here follows prose:

If this fall into thy hand, revolve. In my stars I am above thee, but be not afraid of greatness: some are born great, some a-chieves greatness, and some have greatness thrust upon 'em. Thy fates open their hands, let thy blood and spirit embrace them, and to inure thyself to what thou art like to be: cast thy humble slough, and appear fresh. Be opposite with a kinsman, surly with servants: let thy tongue tang arguments of state; put thyself into the trick of singularity. She thus advises thee, that

*sighs for thee. Remember who commended thy yellow stock-
ings, and wish'd to see thee ever cross-garter'd: I say remember, go to, thou art made if thou desir'st to be so: if not, let me
see thee a steward still, the fellow of servants, and not worthy
to touch Fortune's fingers. Farewell. She that would alter
services with thee,*

> The Fortunate-Unhappy.

Daylight and champain discovers not more: this is open.
I will be proud, I will read politic authors, I will baffle
Sir Toby, I will wash off gross acquaintance, I will be
point-devise, the very man. I do not now fool myself, to
let imagination jade me; for every reason excites to this,
that my Lady loves me. She did commend my yellow
stockings of late, she did praise my leg being cross-garter'd, and in this she manifests herself to my love, and
with a kind of injunction drives me to these habits of her
liking. I thank my stars, I am happy: I will be strange,
stout, in yellow stockings, and cross-garter'd, even with
the swiftness of putting on. Jove, and my stars be praised.
Here is yet a postscript.

*Thou canst not choose but know who I am. If thou entertain'st
my love, let it appear in thy smiling, thy smiles become thee
well. Therefore in my presence still smile, dear my sweet, I
prithee.*

Jove I thank thee, I will smile, I will do everything that
thou wilt have me.

Exit.

FABIAN: I will not give my part of this sport for a pension
of thousands to be paid from the Sophy.

SIR TOBY: I could marry this wench for this device.

SIR ANDREW: So could I too.

SIR TOBY: And ask no other dowry with her, but such another jest.

Enter Maria.

SIR ANDREW: Nor I neither.

FABIAN: Here comes my noble gull-catcher.

SIR TOBY: Wilt thou set thy foot o' my neck?

SIR ANDREW: Or o' mine either?

SIR TOBY: Shall I play my freedom at tray-trip, and become thy bond-slave?

SIR ANDREW: I' faith, or I either?

SIR TOBY: Why, thou hast put him in such a dream, that when the image of it leaves him, he must run mad.

MARIA: Nay but say true, does it work upon him?

SIR TOBY: Like aqua-vitæ with a midwife.

MARIA: If you will then see the fruits of the sport, mark his first approach before my Lady: he will come to her in yellow stockings, and 'tis a colour she abhors, and cross-garter'd, a fashion she detests: and he will smile upon her, which will now be so unsuitable to her disposition, being addicted to a melancholy, as she is, that it cannot but turn him into a notable contempt: if you will see it follow me.

SIR TOBY: To the gates of Tartar, thou most excellent devil of wit.

SIR ANDREW: I'll make one too.

Exeunt.

III. 1

Enter Viola and Clown.

VIOLA: Save thee friend and thy music: dost thou live by thy tabor?

CLOWN: No sir, I live by the Church.

VIOLA: Art thou a churchman?

CLOWN: No such matter sir, I do live by the Church: for,

I do live at my house, and my house doth stand by the Church.

VIOLA: So thou mayst say the King lies by a beggar, if a beggar dwell near him: or the Church stands by thy tabor, if thy tabor stand by the Church.

CLOWN: You have said sir: to see this age: a sentence is but a cheveril glove to a good wit, how quickly the wrong side may be turn'd outward.

VIOLA: Nay that's certain: they that dally nicely with words, may quickly make them wanton.

CLOWN: I would therefore my sister had had no name sir.

VIOLA: Why man?

CLOWN: Why sir, her name's a word, and to dally with that word might make my sister wanton: but indeed, words are very rascals, since bonds disgrac'd them.

VIOLA: Thy reason man?

CLOWN: Troth sir, I can yield you none without words, and words are grown so false, I am loath to prove reason with them.

VIOLA: I warrant thou art a merry fellow, and car'st for nothing.

CLOWN: Not so sir, I do care for something: but in my conscience sir, I do not care for you: if that be to care for nothing sir, I would it would make you invisible.

VIOLA: Art not thou the Lady Olivia's fool?

CLOWN: No indeed sir, the Lady Olivia has no folly, she will keep no fool sir, till she be married, and fools are as like husbands, as pilchers are to herrings, the husband's the bigger, I am indeed not her fool, but her corrupter of words.

VIOLA: I saw thee late at the Count Orsino's.

CLOWN: Foolery sir, does walk about the Orb like the Sun it shines everywhere. I would be sorry sir, but the fool

should be as oft with your master, as with my mistress: I
think I saw your wisdom there.

VIOLA: Nay, and thou pass upon me, I'll no more with
thee. Hold there's expenses for thee.

CLOWN: Now Jove in his next commodity of hair, send
thee a beard.

VIOLA: By my troth I'll tell thee, I am almost sick for one,
though I would not have it grow on my chin. Is thy Lady
within?

CLOWN: Would not a pair of these have bred sir?

VIOLA: Yes being kept together, and put to use.

CLOWN: I would play Lord Pandarus of Phrygia sir, to
bring a Cressida to this Troilus.

VIOLA: I understand you sir, 'tis well begg'd.

CLOWN: The matter I hope is not great sir; begging, but a
beggar: Cressida was a beggar. My Lady is within sir. I
will conster to them whence you come, who you are,
and what you would are out of my welkin, I might say
element, but the word is overworn.

Exit.

VIOLA: This fellow is wise enough to play the fool,
And to do that well, craves a kind of wit:
He must observe their mood on whom he jests,
The quality of persons, and the time:
And like the haggard, check at every feather
That comes before his eye. This is a practice,
As full of labour as a wise man's art:
For folly that he wisely shows, is fit;
But wise men folly-fall'n, quite taint their wit.

Enter Sir Toby and Sir Andrew.

SIR TOBY: Save you gentleman.

VIOLA: And you sir.

SIR ANDREW: *Dieu vous garde Monsieur.*

VIOLA: *Et vous aussi votre serviteur.*

SIR ANDREW: I hope sir, you are, and I am yours.

SIR TOBY: Will you encounter the house, my niece is desirous you should enter, if your trade be to her.

VIOLA: I am bound to your niece sir, I mean she is the list of my voyage.

SIR TOBY: Taste your legs sir, put them to motion.

VIOLA: My legs do better understand me sir, than I understand what you mean by bidding me taste my legs.

SIR TOBY: I mean to go sir, to enter.

VIOLA: I will answer you with gait and entrance, but we are prevented.

Enter Olivia and Gentlewoman.

Most excellent accomplish'd Lady, the heavens rain odours on you.

SIR ANDREW: That youth's a rare Courtier, rain odours, well.

VIOLA: My matter hath no voice Lady, but to your own most pregnant and vouchsafed ear.

SIR ANDREW: Odours, pregnant, and vouchsafed: I'll get 'em all three all ready.

OLIVIA: Let the garden door be shut, and leave me to my hearing. [*Exeunt Sir Toby, Sir Andrew, and Gentlewoman.*] Give me your hand sir.

VIOLA: My duty Madam, and most humble service.

OLIVIA: What is your name?

VIOLA: Cesario is your servant's name, fair Princess.

OLIVIA: My servant sir? 'Twas never merry world, Since lowly feigning was call'd compliment: Y'are servant to the Count Orsino youth.

VIOLA: And he is yours, and his must needs be yours: Your servant's servant, is your servant Madam.

OLIVIA: For him, I think not on him: for his thoughts

Would they were blanks, rather than fill'd with me.

VIOLA: Madam, I come to whet your gentle thoughts
  On his behalf.

OLIVIA: O by your leave I pray you.
  I bade you never speak again of him;
  But would you undertake another suit
  I had rather hear you, to solicit that,
  Than music from the spheres.

VIOLA: Dear Lady.

OLIVIA: Give me leave, beseech you: I did send,
  After the last enchantment you did here,
  A ring in chase of you. So did I abuse
  Myself, my servant, and I fear me you:
  Under your hard construction must I sit,
  To force that on you in a shameful cunning
  Which you knew none of yours. What might you think?
  Have you not set mine honour at the stake,
  And baited it with all th' unmuzzled thoughts
  That tyrannous heart can think? To one of your receiving
  Enough is shown, a cypress, not a bosom,
  Hides my heart: so let me hear you speak.

VIOLA. I pity you.

OLIVIA: That's a degree to love.

VIOLA: No not a grize: for 'tis a vulgar proof
  That very oft we pity enemies.

OLIVIA: Why then methinks 'tis time to smile again:
  O world, how apt the poor are to be proud!
  If one should be a prey, how much the better
  To fall before the lion, than the wolf!
                  Clock strikes.
  The clock upbraids me with the waste of time:
  Be not afraid good youth, I will not have you,
  And yet when wit and youth is come to harvest,

Your wife is like to reap a proper man:
There lies your way, due West.
VIOLA: Then westward-ho:
Grace and good disposition attend your Ladyship:
You'll nothing Madam to my Lord, by me?
OLIVIA: Stay: I prithee tell me what thou think'st of me?
VIOLA: That you do think you are not what you are.
OLIVIA: If I think so, I think the same of you.
VIOLA: Then think you right: I am not what I am.
OLIVIA: I would you were, as I would have you be.
VIOLA: Would it be better, Madam, than I am?
I wish it might, for now I am your fool.
OLIVIA: O what a deal of scorn, looks beautiful!
In the contempt and anger of his lip,
A murderous guilt shows not itself more soon,
Than love that would seem hid: Love's night, is noon.
Cesario, by the roses of the spring,
By maid-hood, honour, truth, and every thing,
I love thee so, that maugre all thy pride,
Nor wit, nor reason, can my passion hide:
Do not extort thy reasons from this clause,
For that I woo, thou therefore hast no cause:
But rather reason thus, with reason fetter;
Love sought, is good: but given unsought, is better.
VIOLA: By innocence I swear, and by my youth,
I have one heart, one bosom, and one truth,
And that no woman has, nor never none
Shall mistress be of it, save I alone.
And so adieu good Madam, never more,
Will I my master's tears to you deplore.
OLIVIA: Yet come again; for thou perhaps mayst move
That heart which now abhors, to like his love.
                    Exeunt.

III. 2

Enter Sir Toby, Sir Andrew, and Fabian.

SIR ANDREW: No faith, I'll not stay a jot longer.

SIR TOBY: Thy reason dear venom, give thy reason.

FABIAN: You must needs yield your reason, Sir Andrew.

SIR ANDREW: Marry I saw your niece do more favours to the Count's serving-man, than ever she bestow'd upon me: I saw't i' th' orchard.

SIR TOBY: Did she see thee the while, old boy, tell me that.

SIR ANDREW: As plain as I see you now.

FABIAN: This was a great argument of love in her toward you.

SIR ANDREW: S'light; will you make an ass o' me?

FABIAN: I will prove it legitimate sir, upon the oaths of judgement, and reason.

SIR TOBY: And they have been grand-jurymen, since before Noah was a sailor.

FABIAN: She did show favour to the youth in your sight, only to exasperate you, to awake your dormouse valour, to put fire in your heart, and brimstone in your liver: you should then have accosted her, and with some excellent jests, fire-new from the mint, you should have bang'd the youth into dumbness: this was look'd for at your hand, and this was balk'd: the double gilt of this opportunity you let time wash off, and you are now sail'd into the North of my Lady's opinion, where you will hang like an icicle on a Dutchman's beard, unless you do redeem it, by some laudable attempt, either of valour or policy.

SIR ANDREW: And't be any way, it must be with valour,

for policy I hate: I had as lief be a Brownist, as a politician.

SIR TOBY: Why then build me thy fortunes upon the basis of valour. Challenge me the Count's youth to fight with him, hurt him in eleven places, my niece shall take note of it, and assure thyself, there is no love-broker in the world, can more prevail in man's commendation with woman, than report of valour.

FABIAN: There is no way but this Sir Andrew.

SIR ANDREW: Will either of you bear me a challenge to him?

SIR TOBY: Go, write it in a martial hand, be curst and brief: it is no matter how witty, so it be eloquent, and full of invention: taunt him with the license of ink: if thou thou'st him some thrice, it shall not be amiss, and as many lies, as will lie in thy sheet of paper, although the sheet were big enough for the bed of Ware in England, set 'em down, go about it. Let there be gall enough in thy ink, though thou write with a goose-pen, no matter: about it.

SIR ANDREW: Where shall I find you?

SIR TOBY: We'll call thee at the Cubiculo: go.

Exit Sir Andrew.

FABIAN: This is a dear manakin to you Sir Toby.

SIR TOBY: I have been dear to him lad, some two thousand strong, or so.

FABIAN: We shall have a rare letter from him; but you'll not deliver't?

SIR TOBY: Never trust me then: and by all means stir on the youth to an answer. I think oxen and wainropes cannot hale them together. For Andrew, if he were open'd, and you find so much blood in his liver, as will clog the foot of a flea, I'll eat the rest of th' anatomy.

FABIAN: And his opposite the youth bears in his visage no great presage of cruelty.

Enter Maria.

SIR TOBY: Look where the youngest wren of nine comes.

MARIA: If you desire the spleen, and will laugh yourselves into stitches, follow me; yond gull Malvolio is turned heathen, a very renegado; for there is no Christian that means to be saved by believing rightly, can ever believe such impossible passages of grossness. He's in yellow stockings.

SIR TOBY: And cross-garter'd?

MARIA: Most villainously: like a pedant that keeps a school i' th' Church: I have dogg'd him like his murtherer. He does obey every point of the letter that I dropp'd, to betray him: he does smile his face into more lines, than is in the new map, with the augmentation of the Indies: you have not seen such a thing as 'tis: I can hardly forbear hurling things at him, I know my Lady will strike him: if she do, he'll smile, and take't for a great favour.

SIR TOBY: Come bring us, bring us where he is.

Exeunt.

III. 3

Enter Sebastian and Antonio.

SEBASTIAN: I would not by my will have troubled you,
But since you make your pleasure of your pains,
I will no further chide you.

ANTONIO: I could not stay behind you: my desire
(More sharp than filed steel) did spur me forth,
And not all love to see you (though so much
As might have drawn one to a longer voyage)
But jealousy, what might befall your travel,

   Being skilless in these parts: which to a stranger,
   Unguided, and unfriended, often prove
   Rough, and unhospitable. My willing love,
   The rather by these arguments of fear
   Set forth in your pursuit.
SEBASTIAN: My kind Antonio,
   I can no other answer make, but thanks,
   And thanks: and ever oft good turns,
   Are shuffl'd off with such uncurrent pay:
   But were my worth, as is my conscience firm,
   You should find better dealing: what's to do?
   Shall we go see the reliques of this town?
ANTONIO: To-morrow sir, best first go see your lodging.
SEBASTIAN: I am not weary, and 'tis long to night:
   I pray you let us satisfy our eyes
   With the memorials, and the things of fame
   That do renown this city.
ANTONIO: Would you'ld pardon me:
   I do not without danger walk these streets.
   Once in a sea-fight 'gainst the Count his galleys,
   I did some service, of such note indeed,
   That were I ta'en here, it would scarce be answer'd.
SEBASTIAN: Belike you slew great number of his people.
ANTONIO: Th' offence is not of such a bloody nature,
   Albeit the quality of the time, and quarrel
   Might well have given us bloody argument:
   It might have since been answer'd in repaying
   What we took from them, which for traffic's sake
   Most of our city did. Only myself stood out,
   For which if I be lapsed in this place
   I shall pay dear.
SEBASTIAN: Do not then walk too open.
ANTONIO: It doth not fit me: hold sir, here's my purse

In the south suburbs at the Elephant
Is best to lodge: I will bespeak our diet,
Whiles you beguile the time, and feed your knowledge
With viewing of the town, there shall you have me.

SEBASTIAN: Why I your purse?

ANTONIO: Haply your eye shall light upon some toy
You have desire to purchase: and your store
I think is not for idle markets, sir.

SEBASTIAN: I'll be your purse-bearer, and leave you
For an hour.

ANTONIO: To th' Elephant.

SEBASTIAN: I do remember.

Exeunt.

III. 4

Enter Olivia and Maria.

OLIVIA: I have sent after him, he says he'll come:
How shall I feast him? What bestow of him?
For youth is bought more oft, than begg'd, or borrow'd.
I speak too loud: Where's Malvolio, he is sad, and civil,
And suits well for a servant with my fortunes,
Where is Malvolio?

MARIA: He's coming Madam:
But in very strange manner. He is sure possess'd Madam.

OLIVIA: Why what's the matter, does he rave?

MARIA: No Madam, he does nothing but smile: your
Ladyship were best to have some guard about you, if he
come, for sure the man is tainted in's wits.

OLIVIA: Go call him hither. [*Enter Malvolio.*]
I am as mad as he,
If sad and merry madness equal be.

How now Malvolio?

MALVOLIO: Sweet Lady, ho, ho.

OLIVIA: Smil'st thou? I sent for thee upon a sad occasion.

MALVOLIO: Sad Lady, I could be sad: this does make some obstruction in the blood: this cross-gartering, but what of that? If it please the eye of one, it is with me as the very true sonnet is: Please one, and please all.

MARIA: Why how dost thou man? what is the matter with thee?

MALVOLIO: Not black in my mind, though yellow in my legs: it did come to his hands, and commands shall be executed. I think we do know the sweet Roman hand.

OLIVIA: Wilt thou go to bed Malvolio?

MALVOLIO: To bed? Ay sweet-heart, and I'll come to thee.

OLIVIA: God comfort thee: why dost thou smile so, and kiss thy hand so oft?

MARIA: How do you Malvolio?

MALVOLIO: At your request: yes nightingales answer daws.

MARIA: Why appear you with this ridiculous boldness before my Lady?

MALVOLIO: Be not afraid of greatness: 'twas well writ.

OLIVIA: What mean'st thou by that Malvolio?

MALVOLIO: Some are born great.

OLIVIA: Ha?

MALVOLIO: Some achieve greatness.

OLIVIA: What say'st thou?

MALVOLIO: And some have greatness thrust upon them.

OLIVIA: Heaven restore thee.

MALVOLIO: Remember who commended thy yellow stockings.

OLIVIA: Thy yellow stockings?

MALVOLIO: And wish'd to see thee cross-garter'd.

OLIVIA: Cross-garter'd?

MALVOLIO: Go to, thou art made, if thou desir'st to be so.

OLIVIA: Am I made?

MALVOLIO: If not, let me see thee a servant still.

OLIVIA: Why this is very midsummer madness.

Enter Servant.

SERVANT: Madam, the young gentleman of the Count Orsino's is return'd, I could hardly entreat him back: he attends your Ladyship's pleasure.

OLIVIA: I'll come to him. [*Exit Servant.*] Good Maria, let this fellow be look'd to. Where's my cousin Toby, let some of my people have a special care of him, I would not have him miscarry for the half of my dowry.

Exeunt Olivia and Maria.

MALVOLIO: O ho, do you come near me now: no worse man than Sir Toby to look to me. This concurs directly with the letter, she sends him on purpose, that I may appear stubborn to him: for she incites me to that in the letter. Cast thy humble slough says she: be opposite with a kinsman, surly with servants, let thy tongue tang with arguments of state, put thyself into the trick of singularity: and consequently sets down the manner how: as a sad face, a reverend carriage, a slow tongue, in the habit of some Sir of note, and so forth. I have lim'd her, but it is Jove's doing, and Jove make me thankful. And when she went away now, Let this fellow be look'd to: fellow? not Malvolio, nor after my degree, but fellow. Why every thing adheres together, that no dram of a scruple, no scruple of a scruple, no obstacle, no incredulous or unsafe circumstance: what can be said? Nothing that can be, can come between me, and the full prospect of my hopes. Well Jove, not I, is the doer of this, and he is to be thanked.

Enter Toby, Fabian and Maria.

SIR TOBY: Which way is he in the name of sanctity. If all the devils of hell be drawn in little, and Legion himself possess'd him, yet I'll speak to him.

FABIAN: Here he is, here he is: how is't with you sir? How is't with you man?

MALVOLIO: Go off, I discard you: let me enjoy my private: go off.

MARIA: Lo, how hollow the fiend speaks within him; did not I tell you? Sir Toby, my Lady prays you to have a care of him.

MALVOLIO: Ah ha, does she so?

SIR TOBY: Go to, go to: peace, peace, we must deal gently with him: let me alone. How do you Malvolio? How is't with you? What man, defy the devil: consider, he's an enemy to mankind.

MALVOLIO: Do you know what you say?

MARIA: La you, and you speak ill of the devil, how he takes it at heart. Pray God he be not bewitch'd.

FABIAN: Carry his water to th' wise woman.

MARIA: Marry and it shall be done to-morrow morning if I live. My Lady would not lose him for more than I'll say.

MALVOLIO: How now mistress?

MARIA: O Lord.

SIR TOBY: Prithee hold thy peace, this is not the way: do you not see you move him? Let me alone with him.

FABIAN: No way but gentleness, gently, gently: the Fiend is rough, and will not be roughly us'd.

SIR TOBY: Why how now my bawcock? how dost thou chuck?

MALVOLIO: Sir.

SIR TOBY: Ay Biddy, come with me. What man, 'tis not for gravity to play at cherry-pit with Satan. Hang him foul collier.

MARIA: Get him to say his prayers, good Sir Toby, get him to pray.

MALVOLIO: My prayers minx.

MARIA: No I warrant you, he will not hear of godliness.

MALVOLIO: Go hang yourselves all: you are idle shallow things, I am not of your element, you shall know more hereafter.

Exit.

SIR TOBY: Is't possible?

FABIAN: If this were played upon a stage now, I could condemn it as an improbable fiction.

SIR TOBY: His very genius hath taken the infection of the device man.

MARIA: Nay pursue him now, lest the device take air, and taint.

FABIAN: Why we shall make him mad indeed.

MARIA: The house will be the quieter.

SIR TOBY: Come, we'll have him in a dark room and bound. My niece is already in the belief that he's mad: we may carry it thus for our pleasure, and his penance, till our very pastime tir'd out of breath, prompt us to have mercy on him: at which time, we will bring the device to the bar and crown thee for a finder of madmen: but see, but see.

Enter Sir Andrew.

FABIAN: More matter for a May morning.

SIR ANDREW: Here's the challenge, read it: I warrant there's vinegar and pepper in't.

FABIAN: Is't so saucy?

SIR ANDREW: Ay, is't? I warrant him: do but read.

SIR TOBY: Give me. *Youth whatsoever thou art, thou art but a scurvy fellow.*

FABIAN: Good, and valiant.

SIR TOBY: *Wonder not, nor admire not in thy mind why I do call thee so, for I will show thee no reason for't.*

FABIAN: A good note, that keeps you from the blow of the Law.

SIR TOBY: *Thou com'st to the Lady Olivia, and in my sight she uses thee kindly: but thou liest in thy throat, that is not the matter I challenge thee for.*

FABIAN: Very brief, and to exceeding good sense – less.

SIR TOBY: *I will waylay thee going home, where if it be thy chance to kill me.*

FABIAN: Good.

SIR TOBY: *Thou kill'st me like a rogue and a villain.*

FABIAN: Still you keep o' th' windy side of the Law: good.

SIR TOBY: *Fare thee well, and God have mercy upon one of our souls. He may have mercy upon mine, but my hope is better, and so look to thyself. Thy friend as thou usest him, and thy sworn enemy,*

> *Andrew Aguecheek.*

If this letter move him not, his legs cannot: I'll give't him.

MARIA: You may have very fit occasion for't: he is now in some commerce with my Lady, and will by and by depart.

SIR TOBY: Go Sir Andrew: scout me for him at the corner of the orchard like a bum-baily: so soon as ever thou seest him, draw, and as thou draw'st, swear horrible: for it comes to pass oft, that a terrible oath, with a swaggering accent sharply twang'd off, gives manhood more approbation, than ever proof itself would have earn'd him. Away.

SIR ANDREW: Nay let me alone for swearing.

Exit.

SIR TOBY: Now will not I deliver his letter: for the behaviour of the young gentleman, gives him out to be of good capacity, and breeding: his employment between his Lord and my niece, confirms no less. Therefore, this letter being so excellently ignorant, will breed no terror in the youth: he will find it comes from a clodpole. But sir, I will deliver his challenge by word of mouth; set upon Aguecheek a notable report of valour, and drive the gentleman (as I know his youth will aptly receive it) into a most hideous opinion of his rage, skill, fury, and impetuosity. This will so fright them both, that they will kill one another by the look, like cockatrices.

Enter Olivia and Viola.

FABIAN: Here he comes with your niece, give them way till he take leave, and presently after him.

SIR TOBY: I will meditate the while upon some horrid message for a challenge.

Exeunt Sir Toby, Fabian, and Maria.

OLIVIA: I have said too much unto a heart of stone,
And laid mine honour too unchary on't:
There's something in me that reproves my fault:
But such a headstrong potent fault it is,
That it but mocks reproof.

VIOLA: With the same haviour that your passion bears,
Goes on my master's grief.

OLIVIA: Here, wear this jewel for me, 'tis my picture:
Refuse it not, it hath no tongue, to vex you:
And I beseech you come again to-morrow.
What shall you ask of me that I'll deny,

That honour, sav'd, may upon asking give.

VIOLA: Nothing but this, your true love for my master.

OLIVIA: How with mine honour may I give him that,
Which I have given to you?

VIOLA: I will acquit you.

OLIVIA: Well, come again to-morrow: fare thee well,
A fiend like thee might bear my soul to hell.

Exit.

Enter Toby and Fabian.

SIR TOBY: Gentleman, God save thee.

VIOLA: And you sir.

SIR TOBY: That defence thou hast, betake thee to't: of
what nature the wrongs are thou hast done him, I know
not: but thy intercepter full of despite, bloody as the
hunter, attends thee at the orchard end: dismount thy
tuck, be yare in thy preparation, for thy assailant is quick,
skilful, and deadly.

VIOLA: You mistake sir I am sure, no man hath any quarrel
to me: my remembrance is very free and clear from any
image of offence done to any man.

SIR TOBY: You'll find it otherwise I assure you: therefore,
if you hold your life at any price, betake you to your
guard: for your opposite hath in him what youth,
strength, skill, and wrath, can furnish man withal.

VIOLA: I pray you sir what is he?

SIR TOBY: He is knight dubb'd with unhatch'd rapier, and
on carpet consideration, but he is a devil in private brawl,
souls and bodies hath he divorc'd three, and his incense-
ment at this moment is so implacable, that satisfaction can
be none, but by pangs of death and sepulchre: Hob, nob,
is his word: give't or take't.

VIOLA: I will return again into the house, and desire some
conduct of the Lady. I am no fighter, I have heard of

some kind of men, that put quarrels purposely on others, to taste their valour: belike this is a man of that quirk.

SIR TOBY: Sir, no: his indignation derives itself out of a very competent injury, therefore get you on, and give him his desire. Back you shall not to the house, unless you undertake that with me, which with as much safety you might answer him: therefore on, or strip your sword stark naked: for meddle you must that's certain, or forswear to wear iron about you.

VIOLA: This is as uncivil as strange. I beseech you do me this courteous office, as to know of the Knight what my offence to him is: it is something of my negligence, nothing of my purpose.

SIR TOBY: I will do so. Signior Fabian, stay you by this gentleman, till my return.

Exit,

VIOLA: Pray you sir, do you know of this matter?

FABIAN: I know the knight is incens'd against you, even to a mortal arbitrement, but nothing of the circumstance more.

VIOLA: I beseech you what manner of man is he?

FABIAN: Nothing of that wonderful promise to read him by his form, as you are like to find him in the proof of his valour. He is indeed sir, the most skilful, bloody, and fatal opposite that you could possibly have found in any part of Illyria: will you walk towards him, I will make your peace with him, if I can.

VIOLA: I shall be much bound to you for't: I am one, that had rather go with Sir Priest than Sir Knight: I care not who knows so much of my mettle.

Exeunt.
Enter Toby and Andrew.

SIR TOBY: Why man he's a very devil, I have not seen such

a firago: I had a pass with him, rapier, scabbard, and all: and he gives me the stuck in with such a mortal motion that it is inevitable: and on the answer, he pays you as surely, as your feet hits the ground they step on. They say, he has been fencer to the Sophy.

SIR ANDREW: Pox on't, I'll not meddle with him.

SIR TOBY: Ay but he will not now be pacified, Fabian can scarce hold him yonder.

SIR ANDREW: Plague on't, and I thought he had been valiant, and so cunning in fence, I'd have seen him damn'd ere I'd have challeng'd him. Let him let the matter slip, and I'll give him my horse, grey Capilet.

SIR TOBY: I'll make the motion: stand here, make a good show on't, this shall end without the perdition of souls. Marry I'll ride your horse as well as I ride you.

Enter Fabian and Viola.

I have his horse to take up the quarrel, I have persuaded him the youth's a devil.

FABIAN: He is as horribly conceited of him: and pants, and looks pale, as if a bear were at his heels.

SIR TOBY: There's no remedy sir, he will fight with you for's oath's sake: marry he hath better bethought him of his quarrel, and he finds that now scarce to be worth talking of: therefore draw for the supportance of his vow, he protests he will not hurt you.

VIOLA: Pray God defend me: a little thing would make me tell them how much I lack of a man.

FABIAN: Give ground if you see him furious.

SIR TOBY: Come Sir Andrew, there's no remedy, the gentleman will for his honour's sake have one bout with you: he cannot by the Duello avoid it: but he has promised me, as he is a gentleman and a soldier, he will not hurt you. Come on, to't.

SIR ANDREW: Pray God he keep his oath.
                    Enter Antonio.
VIOLA: I do assure you 'tis against my will.
                    They draw.
ANTONIO: Put up your sword: if this young gentleman
   Have done offence, I take the fault on me:
   If you offend him, I for him defy you.
SIR TOBY: You sir? Why, what are you?
ANTONIO: One sir, that for his love dares yet do more
   Than you have heard him brag to you he will.
SIR TOBY: Nay, if you be an undertaker, I am for you.
                    They draw,
                    Enter Officers,
FABIAN: O good Sir Toby hold: here come the officers.
SIR TOBY: I'll be with you anon.
VIOLA: Pray sir, put your sword up if you please.
SIR ANDREW: Marry will I sir: and for that I promis'd you
   I'll be as good as my word. He will bear you easily, and
   reins well.
1 OFFICER: This is the man, do thy office.
2 OFFICER: Antonio, I arrest thee at the suit of Count Or-
   sino.
ANTONIO: You do mistake me sir.
1 OFFICER: No sir, no jot: I know your favour well:
   Though now you have no sea-cap on your head:
   Take him away, he knows I know him well.
ANTONIO: I must obey. This comes with seeking you:
   But there's no remedy, I shall answer it:
   What will you do: now my necessity
   Makes me to ask you for my purse. It grieves me
   Much more, for what I cannot do for you,
   Than what befalls myself: you stand amaz'd,
   But be of comfort.

2 OFFICER: Come sir away.

ANTONIO: I must entreat of you some of that money.

VIOLA: What money sir?
For the fair kindness you have show'd me here,
And part being prompted by your present trouble,
Out of my lean and low ability
I'll lend you something: my having is not much,
I'll make division of my present with you:
Hold, there's half my coffer.

ANTONIO: Will you deny me now,
Is't possible that my deserts to you
Can lack persuasion? Do not tempt my misery,
Lest that it make me so unsound a man
As to upbraid you with those kindnesses
That I have done for you.

VIOLA: I know of none,
Nor know I you by voice, or any feature:
I hate ingratitude more in a man,
Than lying, vainness, babbling drunkenness,
Or any taint of vice, whose strong corruption
Inhabits our frail blood.

ANTONIO: Oh heavens themselves.

2 OFFICER: Come sir, I pray you go.

ANTONIO: Let me speak a little. This youth that you see
here,
I snatch'd one half out of the jaws of death,
Reliev'd him with such sanctity of love;
And to his image, which methought did promise
Most venerable worth, did I devotion.

1 OFFICER: What's that to us, the time goes by: away.

ANTONIO: But oh, how vile an idol proves this god:
Thou hast Sebastian done good feature, shame.
In Nature, there's no blemish but the mind:

None can be call'd deform'd, but the unkind.
Virtue is beauty, but the beauteous evil
Are empty trunks, o'erflourish'd by the devil.

1 OFFICER: The man grows mad, away with him: come,
come sir.

ANTONIO: Lead me on.

Exit with Officers.

VIOLA: Methinks his words do from such passion fly
That he believes himself, so do not I:
Prove true imagination, oh prove true,
That I dear brother, be now ta'en for you.

SIR TOBY: Come hither Knight, come hither Fabian: we'll
whisper o'er a couplet or two of most sage saws.

VIOLA: He nam'd Sebastian: I my brother know
Yet living in my glass: even such, and so
In favour was my brother, and he went
Still in this fashion, colour, ornament,
For him I imitate: O if it prove,
Tempests are kind, and salt waves fresh in love.

Exit.

SIR TOBY: A very dishonest paltry boy, and more a coward than a hare, his dishonesty appears, in leaving his
friend here in necessity, and denying him: and for his
cowardship ask Fabian.

FABIAN: A coward, a most devout coward, religious in it.

SIR ANDREW: 'Slid I'll after him again, and beat him.

SIR TOBY: Do, cuff him soundly, but never draw thy
sword.

SIR ANDREW: And I do not.

Exit.

FABIAN: Come, let's see the event.

SIR TOBY: I dare lay any money, 'twill be nothing yet.

Exeunt.

IV. 1

Enter Sebastian and Clown.

CLOWN: Will you make me believe, that I am not sent for
you?

SEBASTIAN: Go to, go to, thou art a foolish fellow, let me
be clear of thee.

CLOWN: Well held out i' faith: no, I do not know you, nor
I am not sent to you by my Lady, to bid you come speak
with her: nor your name is not Master Cesario, nor this
is not my nose neither: nothing that is so, is so.

SEBASTIAN: I prithee vent thy folly somewhere else, thou
know'st not me.

CLOWN: Vent my folly: he has heard that word of some
great man, and now applies it to a fool. Vent my folly:
I am afraid this great lubber theWorld will prove a Cockney: I prithee now ungird thy strangeness, and tell me
what I shall vent to my Lady? Shall I vent to her that
thou art coming?

SEBASTIAN: I prithee foolish Greek depart from me.
There's money for thee, if you tarry longer, I shall give
worse payment.

CLOWN: By my troth thou hast an open hand: these wise
men that give fools money, get themselves a good report,
after fourteen years' purchase.

Enter Andrew, Toby, and Fabian.

SIR ANDREW: Now sir, have I met you again: there's for
you.

SEBASTIAN: Why there's for thee, and there, and there.
Are all the people mad?

SIR TOBY: Hold sir, or I'll throw your dagger o'er the
house.

CLOWN: This will I tell my Lady straight, I would not be in some of your coats for two pence.

Exit.

SIR TOBY: Come on sir, hold.

SIR ANDREW: Nay let him alone, I'll go another way to work with him: I'll have an action of battery against him, if there be any law in Illyria: though I struck him first, yet it's no matter for that.

SEBASTIAN: Let go thy hand.

SIR TOBY: Come sir, I will not let you go. Come my young soldier put up your iron: you are well flesh'd: come on.

SEBASTIAN: I will be free from thee. What wouldst thou now?
If thou dar'st tempt me further, draw thy sword.

SIR TOBY: What, what? Nay then I must have an ounce or two of this malapert blood from you.

Enter Olivia.

OLIVIA: Hold Toby, on thy life I charge thee hold.

SIR TOBY: Madam.

OLIVIA: Will it be ever thus? Ungracious wretch,
Fit for the mountains, and the barbarous caves,
Where manners ne'er were preach'd: out of my sight.
Be not offended, dear Cesario:
Rudesby be gone.

Exeunt Sir Toby, Sir Andrew, and Fabian.

I prithee gentle friend,
Let thy fair wisdom, not thy passion sway
In this uncivil, and unjust extent
Against thy peace. Go with me to my house,
And hear thou there how many fruitless pranks
This ruffian hath botch'd up, that thou thereby
Mayst smile at this: thou shalt not choose but go:

Do not deny, beshrew his soul for me,
He started one poor heart of mine, in thee.

SEBASTIAN: What relish is in this? How runs the stream?
Or I am mad, or else this is a dream:
Let fancy still my sense in Lethe steep,
If it be thus to dream, still let me sleep.

OLIVIA: Nay come I prithee, would thou'ldst be rul'd by
me.

SEBASTIAN: Madam, I will.

OLIVIA: O say so, and so be.

Exeunt.

IV. 2

Enter Maria and Clown.

MARIA: Nay, I prithee put on this gown, and this beard,
make him believe thou art Sir Topas the Curate: do it
quickly. I'll call Sir Toby the whilst.

Exit.

CLOWN: Well, I'll put it on, and I will dissemble myself
in't, and I would I were the first that ever dissembled in
such a gown. I am not tall enough to become the function well, nor lean enough to be thought a good student:
but to be said an honest man and a good housekeeper
goes as fairly, as to say, a careful man, and a great scholar.
The competitors enter.

Enter Toby and Maria.

SIR TOBY: Jove bless thee Master Parson.

CLOWN: *Bonos dies* Sir Toby: for as the old hermit of
Prague that never saw pen and ink, very wittily said to
a niece of King Gorboduc, That that is, is: so I being
Master Parson, am Master Parson: for what is that, but
that? and is, but is?

SIR TOBY: To him Sir Topas.

CLOWN: What hoa, I say, Peace in this prison.

SIR TOBY: The knave counterfeits well: a good knave.

Malvolio within.

MALVOLIO: Who calls there?

CLOWN: Sir Topas the Curate, who comes to visit Malvolio the lunatic.

MALVOLIO: Sir Topas, Sir Topas, good Sir Topas go to my Lady.

CLOWN: Out hyperbolical fiend, how vexest thou this man? Talkest thou nothing but of Ladies?

SIR TOBY: Well said Master Parson.

MALVOLIO: Sir Topas, never was man thus wronged, good Sir Topas do not think I am mad: they have laid me here in hideous darkness.

CLOWN: Fie, thou dishonest Satan: I call thee by the most modest terms, for I am one of those gentle ones, that will use the devil himself with courtesy: sayest thou that house is dark?

MALVOLIO: As hell Sir Topas.

CLOWN: Why, it hath bay windows transparent as barricadoes, and the clearstores toward the south north, are as lustrous as ebony: and yet complainest thou of obstruction?

MALVOLIO: I am not mad Sir Topas, I say to you this house is dark.

CLOWN: Madman thou errest: I say there is no darkness but ignorance, in which thou art more puzzl'd than the Egyptians in their fog.

MALVOLIO: I say this house is as dark as ignorance, though ignorance were as dark as hell; and I say there was never man thus abus'd, I am no more mad than you are, make the trial of it in any constant question.

CLOWN: What is the opinion of Pythagoras concerning wild fowl?

MALVOLIO: That the soul of our grandam, might happily inhabit a bird.

CLOWN: What thinkest thou of his opinion?

MALVOLIO: I think nobly of the soul, and no way approve his opinion.

CLOWN: Fare thee well: remain thou still in darkness, thou shalt hold th' opinion of Pythagoras, ere I will allow of thy wits, and fear to kill a woodcock, lest thou dispossess the soul of thy grandam. Fare thee well.

MALVOLIO: Sir Topas, Sir Topas.

SIR TOBY: My most exquisite Sir Topas.

CLOWN: Nay I am for all waters.

MARIA: Thou mightst have done this without thy beard and gown, he sees thee not.

SIR TOBY: To him in thine own voice, and bring me word how thou find'st him: I would we were well rid of this knavery. If he may be conveniently deliver'd, I would he were, for I am now so far in offence with my niece, that I cannot pursue with any safety this sport the upshot. Come by and by to my chamber.

Exeunt Sir Toby and Maria.

CLOWN: Hey Robin, jolly Robin,
　　　　Tell me how thy Lady does.

MALVOLIO: Fool.

CLOWN: My Lady is unkind, perdy.

MALVOLIO: Fool.

CLOWN: Alas why is she so?

MALVOLIO: Fool, I say.

CLOWN: She loves another. Who calls, ha?

MALVOLIO: Good fool, as ever thou wilt deserve well at my hand, help me to a candle, and pen, ink, and paper:

as I am a gentleman, I will live to be thankful to thee
for't.

CLOWN: Master Malvolio?

MALVOLIO: Ay good fool.

CLOWN: Alas sir, how fell you besides your five wits?

MALVOLIO: Fool, there was never man so notoriously a-
bus'd: I am as well in my wits, fool, as thou art.

CLOWN: But as well: then you are mad indeed, if you be
no better in your wits than a fool.

MALVOLIO: They have here propertied me: keep me in
darkness, send ministers to me, asses, and do all they can
to face me out of my wits.

CLOWN: Advise you what you say: the minister is here.
Malvolio, Malvolio, thy wits the heavens restore: endea-
vour thyself to sleep, and leave thy vain bibble babble.

MALVOLIO: Sir Topas.

CLOWN: Maintain no words with him good fellow. Who
I sir, not I sir. God buy you good Sir Topas. Marry amen.
I will, sir, I will.

MALVOLIO: Fool, fool, fool I say.

CLOWN: Alas sir be patient. What say you sir, I am shent
for speaking to you.

MALVOLIO: Good fool, help me to some light, and some
paper, I tell thee I am as well in my wits, as any man in
Illyria.

CLOWN: Well-a-day, that you were sir.

MALVOLIO: By this hand I am: good fool, some ink,
paper, and light: and convey what I will set down to my
Lady: it shall advantage thee more, than ever the bearing
of letter did.

CLOWN: I will help you to't. But tell me true, are you not
mad indeed, or do you but counterfeit?

MALVOLIO: Believe me I am not, I tell thee true.

CLOWN: Nay, I'll ne'er believe a madman till I see his brains. I will fetch you light, and paper, and ink.

MALVOLIO: Fool, I'll requite it in the highest degree: I prithee be gone.

CLOWN: I am gone sir, and anon sir,
　　　　I'll be with you again:
　　　　　In a trice, like to the old Vice,
　　　　Your need to sustain.
　　　　Who with dagger of lath, in his rage and his
　　　　　wrath,
　　　　　Cries ah ha, to the devil:
　　　　Like a mad lad, pare thy nails dad,
　　　　　Adieu good man devil.
　　　　　　　　　Exit.

IV. 3

Enter Sebastian.

SEBASTIAN: This is the air, that is the glorious Sun,
This pearl she gave me, I do feel't, and see't,
And though 'tis wonder that enwraps me thus,
Yet 'tis not madness. Where's Antonio then,
I could not find him at the Elephant,
Yet there he was, and there I found this credit,
That he did range the town to seek me out,
His counsel now might do me golden service,
For though my soul disputes well with my sense,
That this may be some error, but no madness,
Yet doth this accident and flood of Fortune,
So far exceed all instance, all discourse,
That I am ready to distrust mine eyes,
And wrangle with my reason that persuades me
To any other trust, but that I am mad,

Or else the Lady's mad; yet if 'twere so,
She could not sway her house, command her followers,
Take, and give back affairs, and their dispatch,
With such a smooth, discreet, and stable bearing
As I perceive she does: there's something in't
That is deceivable. But here the Lady comes.

Enter Olivia and Priest.

OLIVIA: Blame not this haste of mine: if you mean well
Now go with me, and with this holy man
Into the Chantry by: there before him,
And underneath that consecrated roof,
Plight me the full assurance of your faith,
That my most jealous, and too doubtful soul
May live at peace. He shall conceal it,
Whiles you are willing it shall come to note,
What time we will our celebration keep
According to my birth, what do you say?

SEBASTIAN: I'll follow this good man, and go with you,
And having sworn truth, ever will be true.

OLIVIA: Then lead the way good father, and heavens so shine,
That they may fairly note this act of mine.

Exeunt.

V. I

Enter Clown and Fabian.

FABIAN: Now as thou lov'st me, let me see his letter.

CLOWN: Good Master Fabian, grant me another request.

FABIAN: Any thing.

CLOWN: Do not desire to see this letter.

FABIAN: This is to give a dog, and in recompense desire my dog again.

Enter Duke, Viola, Curio, and Lords.

DUKE: Belong you to the Lady Olivia, friends?

CLOWN: Ay sir, we are some of her trappings.

DUKE: I know thee well: how doest thou my good fellow?

CLOWN: Truly sir, the better for my foes, and the worse for my friends.

DUKE: Just the contrary: the better for thy friends.

CLOWN: No sir, the worse.

DUKE: How can that be?

CLOWN: Marry sir, they praise me, and make an ass of me, now my foes tell me plainly, I am an ass: so that by my foes sir, I profit in the knowledge of myself, and by my friends I am abused: so that conclusions to be as kisses, if your four negatives make your two affirmatives, why then the worse for my friends, and the better for my foes.

DUKE: Why this is excellent.

CLOWN: By my troth sir, no: though it please you to be one of my friends.

DUKE: Thou shalt not be the worse for me, there's gold.

CLOWN: But that it would be double dealing sir, I would you could make it another.

DUKE: O you give me ill counsel.

CLOWN: Put your grace in your pocket sir, for this once, and let your flesh and blood obey it.

DUKE: Well, I will be so much a sinner to be a double dealer: there's another.

CLOWN: *Primo, secundo, tertio,* is a good play, and the old saying is, the third pays for all: the triplex sir, is a good tripping measure, or the bells of Saint Bennet sir, may put you in mind, one, two, three.

DUKE: You can fool no more money out of me at this throw: if you will let your Lady know I am here to speak

with her, and bring her along with you, it may awake
my bounty further.

CLOWN: Marry sir, lullaby to your bounty till I come a-
gain. I go sir, but I would not have you to think, that my
desire of having is the sin of covetousness: but as you say
sir, let your bounty take a nap, I will awake it anon.

Exit.

Enter Antonio and Officers.

VIOLA: Here comes the man sir, that did rescue me.

DUKE: That face of his I do remember well,
Yet when I saw it last, it was besmear'd
As black as Vulcan, in the smoke of war:
A bawbling vessel was he captain of,
For shallow draught and bulk unprizable,
With which such scathful grapple did he make,
With the most noble bottom of our fleet,
That very envy, and the tongue of loss
Cried fame and honour on him: what's the matter?

I OFFICER: Orsino, this is that Antonio
That took the *Phœnix*, and her fraught from Candy,
And this is he that did the *Tiger* board,
When your young nephew Titus lost his leg;
Here in the streets, desperate of shame and state,
In private brabble did we apprehend him.

VIOLA: He did me kindness sir, drew on my side,
But in conclusion put strange speech upon me,
I know not what 'twas, but distraction.

DUKE: Notable pirate, thou salt-water thief,
What foolish boldness brought thee to their mercies,
Whom thou in terms so bloody, and so dear
Hast made thine enemies?

ANTONIO: Orsino: noble sir,
Be pleas'd that I shake off these names you give me:

Antonio never yet was thief, or pirate,
Though I confess, on base and ground enough
Orsino's enemy. A witchcraft drew me hither:
That most ingrateful boy there by your side,
From the rude sea's enrag'd and foamy mouth
Did I redeem: a wrack past hope he was:
His life I gave him, and did thereto add
My love without retention, or restraint,
All his in dedication. For his sake,
Did I expose myself (pure for his love)
Into the danger of this adverse town,
Drew to defend him, when he was beset:
Where being apprehended, his false cunning
(Not meaning to partake with me in danger)
Taught him to face me out of his acquaintance,
And grew a twenty years removed thing
While one would wink: denied me mine own purse,
Which I had recommended to his use,
Not half an hour before.

VIOLA: How can this be?

DUKE: When came he to this town?

ANTONIO: To-day my Lord: and for three months before,
No interim, not a minute's vacancy,
Both day and night did we keep company.

Enter Olivia and Attendants.

DUKE: Here comes the Countess, now heaven walks on
earth:
But for thee fellow, fellow thy words are madness,
Three months this youth hath tended upon me,
But more of that anon. Take him aside.

OLIVIA: What would my Lord, but that he may not have,
Wherein Olivia may seem serviceable?
Cesario, you do not keep promise with me.

VIOLA: Madam.

DUKE: Gracious Olivia.

OLIVIA: What do you say Cesario? Good my Lord.

VIOLA: My Lord would speak, my duty hushes me.

OLIVIA: If it be aught to the old tune my Lord,
    It is as fat and fulsome to mine ear
    As howling after music.

DUKE: Still so cruel?

OLIVIA: Still so constant, Lord.

DUKE: What to perverseness? you uncivil Lady
    To whose ingrate, and unauspicious altars
    My soul the faithfull'st offerings hath breath'd out
    That e'er devotion tender'd. What shall I do?

OLIVIA: Even what it please my Lord, that shall become
    him.

DUKE: Why should I not, (had I the heart to do it)
    Like to th' Egyptian thief, at point of death
    Kill what I love: a savage jealousy,
    That sometime savours nobly: but hear me this:
    Since you to non-regardance cast my faith,
    And that I partly know the instrument
    That screws me from my true place in your favour:
    Live you the marble-breasted tyrant still.
    But this your minion, whom I know you love,
    And whom, by heaven I swear, I tender dearly,
    Him will I tear out of that cruel eye,
    Where he sits crowned in his master's spite.
    Come boy with me, my thoughts are ripe in mischief:
    I'll sacrifice the lamb that I do love,
    To spite a raven's heart within a dove.

VIOLA: And I most jocund, apt, and willingly,
    To do you rest, a thousand deaths would die.

OLIVIA: Where goes Cesario?

VIOLA: After him I love,
  More than I love these eyes, more than my life,
  More by all mores, than e'er I shall love wife.
  If I do feign, you witnesses above
  Punish my life, for tainting of my love.
OLIVIA: Ay me detested, how am I beguil'd?
VIOLA: Who does beguile you? who does do you wrong?
OLIVIA: Hast thou forgot thyself? Is it so long?
  Call forth the holy Father.
DUKE: Come, away.
OLIVIA: Whither my Lord? Cesario, husband, stay.
DUKE: Husband?
OLIVIA: Ay husband. Can he that deny?
DUKE: Her husband, sirrah?
VIOLA: No my Lord, not I.
OLIVIA: Alas, it is the baseness of thy fear,
  That makes thee strangle thy propriety:
  Fear not Cesario, take thy fortunes up,
  Be that thou know'st thou art, and then thou art
  As great as that thou fear'st.

Enter Priest.

  O welcome Father:
  Father, I charge thee by thy reverence
  Here to unfold, though lately we intended
  To keep in darkness, what occasion now
  Reveals before 'tis ripe: what thou dost know
  Hath newly pass'd, between this youth, and me.
PRIEST: A contract of eternal bond of love,
  Confirm'd by mutual joinder of your hands,
  Attested by the holy close of lips,
  Strengthen'd by interchangement of your rings,
  And all the ceremony of this compact
  Seal'd in my function, by my testimony:

Since when, my watch hath told me, toward my grave
I have travell'd but two hours.

DUKE: O thou dissembling cub: what wilt thou be
When time hath sow'd a grizzle on thy case?
Or will not else thy craft so quickly grow,
That thine own trip shall be thine overthrow:
Farewell, and take her, but direct thy feet,
Where thou, and I henceforth may never meet.

VIOLA: My Lord, I do protest.

OLIVIA: O do not swear,
Hold little faith, though thou hast too much fear.

Enter Sir Andrew.

SIR ANDREW: For the love of God a surgeon, send one
presently to Sir Toby.

OLIVIA: What's the matter?

SIR ANDREW: Has broke my head across, and has given
Sir Toby a bloody coxcomb too: for the love of God
your help, I had rather than forty pound I were at home.

OLIVIA: Who has done this Sir Andrew?

SIR ANDREW: The Count's gentleman, one Cesario: we
took him for a coward, but he's the very devil incardinate.

DUKE: My gentleman Cesario?

SIR ANDREW: 'Od's lifelings here he is: you broke my
head for nothing, and that that I did, I was set on to do't
by Sir Toby.

VIOLA: Why do you speak to me? I never hurt you:
You drew your sword upon me without cause,
But I bespake you fair, and hurt you not.

Enter Sir Toby and Clown.

SIR ANDREW: If a bloody coxcomb be a hurt, you have
hurt me: I think you set nothing by a bloody coxcomb.
Here comes Sir Toby halting, you shall hear more: but if

he had not been in drink, he would have tickl'd you
othergates than he did.

DUKE: How now gentleman? how is't with you?

SIR TOBY: That's all one, has hurt me, and there's th' end
on't: sot, didst see Dick Surgeon, sot?

CLOWN: O he's drunk Sir Toby an hour agone: his eyes
were set at eight i' th' morning.

SIR TOBY: Then he's a rogue, and a passy measures pavin:
I hate a drunken rogue.

OLIVIA: Away with him! Who hath made this havoc with
them?

SIR ANDREW: I'll help you Sir Toby, because we'll be
dress'd together.

SIR TOBY: Will you help an ass-head, and a coxcomb, and
a knave: a thin fac'd knave, a gull?

OLIVIA: Get him to bed, and let his hurt be look'd to.
        Exeunt Clown, Fabian, Sir Toby, and Sir Andrew.
                    Enter Sebastian.

SEBASTIAN: I am sorry Madam I have hurt your kinsman:
But had it been the brother of my blood,
I must have done no less with wit and safety.
You throw a strange regard upon me, and by that
I do perceive it hath offended you:
Pardon me, sweet one, even for the vows
We made each other, but so late ago.

DUKE: One face, one voice, one habit, and two persons,
A natural perspective, that is, and is not.

SEBASTIAN: Antonio: O my dear Antonio,
How have the hours rack'd, and tortur'd me,
Since I have lost thee?

ANTONIO: Sebastian are you?

SEBASTIAN: Fear'st thou that Antonio?

ANTONIO: How have you made division of yourself?

An apple cleft in two, is not more twin
Than these two creatures. Which is Sebastian?
OLIVIA: Most wonderful.
SEBASTIAN: Do I stand there? I never had a brother:
  Nor can there be that deity in my nature
  Of here, and every where. I had a sister,
  Whom the blind waves and surges have devour'd:
  Of charity, what kin are you to me?
  What countryman? What name? What parentage?
VIOLA: Of Messaline: Sebastian was my father,
  Such a Sebastian was my brother too:
  So went he suited to his watery tomb:
  If spirits can assume both form and suit,
  You come to fright us.
SEBASTIAN: A spirit I am indeed,
  But am in that dimension grossly clad,
  Which from the womb I did participate.
  Were you a woman, as the rest goes even,
  I should my tears let fall upon your cheek,
  And say, Thrice-welcome drowned Viola.
VIOLA: My father had a mole upon his brow.
SEBASTIAN: And so had mine.
VIOLA: And died that day when Viola from her birth
  Had numbered thirteen years.
SEBASTIAN: O that record is lively in my soul,
  He finished indeed his mortal act
  That day that made my sister thirteen years.
VIOLA: If nothing lets to make us happy both,
  But this my masculine usurp'd attire:
  Do not embrace me, till each circumstance,
  Of place, time, fortune, do cohere and jump
  That I am Viola, which to confirm,
  I'll bring you to a captain in this town,

Where lie my maiden weeds: by whose gentle help,
I was preserv'd to serve this noble Count:
All the occurrence of my fortune since
Hath been between this Lady, and this Lord.

SEBASTIAN: So comes it Lady, you have been mistook:
But Nature to her bias drew in that.
You would have been contracted to a maid,
Nor are you therein (by my life) deceiv'd,
You are betroth'd both to a maid and man.

DUKE: Be not amaz'd, right noble is his blood:
If this be so, as yet the glass seems true,
I shall have share in this most happy wrack:
Boy, thou hast said to me a thousand times,
Thou never shouldst love woman like to me.

VIOLA: And all those sayings, will I over-swear,
And all those swearings keep as true in soul,
As doth that orbed continent, the fire,
That severs day from night.

DUKE: Give me thy hand,
And let me see thee in thy woman's weeds.

VIOLA: The captain that did bring me first on shore
Hath my maid's garments: he upon some action
Is now in durance, at Malvolio's suit,
A gentleman, and follower of my Lady's.

OLIVIA: He shall enlarge him: fetch Malvolio hither,
And yet alas, now I remember me,
They say poor gentleman, he's much distract.

Enter Clown with a letter, and Fabian.

A most extracting frenzy of mine own
From my remembrance, clearly banish'd his.
How does he sirrah?

CLOWN: Truly Madam, he holds Belzebub at the stave's
end as well as a man in his case may do: has here writ a

letter to you, I should have given't you to-day morning.
But as a madman's Epistles are no Gospels, so it skills not
much when they are deliver'd.

OLIVIA: Open't, and read it.

CLOWN: Look then to be well edified, when the fool de-
livers the madman. *By the Lord Madam.*

OLIVIA: How now, art thou mad?

CLOWN: No Madam, I do but read madness: and your
Ladyship will have it as it ought to be, you must allow *Vox.*

OLIVIA: Prithee read i' thy right wits.

CLOWN: So I do Madonna: but to read his right wits, is to
read thus: therefore, perpend my Princess, and give ear.

OLIVIA: Read it you, sirrah.

FABIAN [*reads*]: *By the Lord Madam, you wrong me, and the
world shall know it: though you have put me into darkness,
and given your drunken cousin rule over me, yet have I the
benefit of my senses as well as your Ladyship. I have your own
letter, that induced me to the s m lance I put on; with the
which I doubt not, but to do myself much right, or you much
shame: think of me as you please. I leave my duty a little un-
thought of, and speak out of my injury.*

The madly-us'd Malvolio.

OLIVIA: Did he write this?

CLOWN: Ay Madam.

DUKE: This savours not much of distraction.

OLIVIA: See him deliver'd Fabian, bring him hither:

Exit Fabian.

My Lord, so please you, these things further thought on,
To think me as well a sister, as a wife,
One day shall crown th' alliance on't, so please you,
Here at my house, and at my proper cost.

DUKE: Madam, I am most apt t' embrace your offer:
Your master quits you: and for your service done him,

So much against the mettle of your sex,
So far beneath your soft and tender breeding,
And since you call'd me master for so long:
Here is my hand, you shall from this time be
Your master's mistress.

OLIVIA: A sister, you are she.

Enter Malvolio and Fabian.

DUKE: Is this the madman?

OLIVIA: Ay my Lord, this same: how now Malvolio?

MALVOLIO: Madam, you have done me wrong,
Notorious wrong.

OLIVIA: Have I Malvolio? No.

MALVOLIO: Lady you have, pray you peruse that letter.
You must not now deny it is your hand,
Write from it if you can, in hand, or phrase,
Or say, 'tis not your seal, not your invention:
You can say none of this. Well, grant it then,
And tell me in the modesty of honour,
Why you have given me such clear lights of favour,
Bade me come smiling, and cross-garter'd to you,
To put on yellow stockings, and to frown
Upon Sir Toby, and the lighter people:
And acting this in an obedient hope,
Why have you suffer'd me to be imprison'd,
Kept in a dark house, visited by the Priest,
And made the most notorious geck and gull,
That e'er invention play'd on? Tell me why?

OLIVIA: Alas Malvolio, this is not my writing,
Though I confess much like the character:
But out of question, 'tis Maria's hand.
And now I do bethink me, it was she
First told me thou wast mad; then cam'st in smiling,
And in such forms, which here were presuppos'd

Upon thee in the letter: prithee be content,
This practice hath most shrewdly pass'd upon thee:
But when we know the grounds, and authors of it,
Thou shalt be both the plaintiff and the judge
Of thine own cause.

FABIAN: Good Madam hear me speak,
And let no quarrel, nor no brawl to come,
Taint the condition of this present hour,
Which I have wonder'd at. In hope it shall not,
Most freely I confess myself, and Toby
Set this device against Malvolio here,
Upon some stubborn and uncourteous parts
We had conceiv'd against him. Maria writ
The letter, at Sir Toby's great importance,
In recompense whereof, he hath married her:
How with a sportful malice it was follow'd,
May rather pluck on laughter than revenge,
If that the injuries be justly weigh'd,
That have on both sides pass'd.

OLIVIA: Alas poor fool, how have they baffled thee?

CLOWN: Why some are born great, some achieve greatness, and some have greatness thrown upon them. I was
one sir, in this interlude, one Sir Topas sir, but that's all
one: by the Lord fool, I am not mad: but do you remember, Madam, why laugh you at such a barren rascal, and
you smile not he's gagg'd: and thus the whirligig of time
brings in his revenges

MALVOLIO: I'll be reveng'd on the whole pack of you!
Exit.

OLIVIA: He hath been most notoriously abus'd.

DUKE: Pursue him, and entreat him to a peace:
He hath not told us of the captain yet,
When that is known, and golden time convents,

A solemn combination shall be made
Of our dear souls. Meantime sweet sister,
We will not part from hence. Cesario come
(For so you shall be while you are a man)
But when in other habits you are seen,
Orsino's Mistress, and his fancy's Queen.

Exeunt all but Clown.

CLOWN [*sings*]:

When that I was and a little tiny boy,
    With hey ho, the wind and the rain:
A foolish thing was but a toy,
    For the rain it raineth every day.

But when I came to man's estate.
    With hey ho, &c.
'Gainst knaves and thieves men shut their gate,
    For the rain, &c.

But when I came alas to wive,
    With hey ho, &c.
By swaggering could I never thrive,
    For the rain, &c.

But when I came unto my beds,
    With hey ho, &c.
With toss-pots still had drunken heads,
    For the rain, &c.

A great while ago the world begun,
    With hey ho, &c.
But that's all one, our Play is done,
    And we'll strive to please you every day.

Exit.

NOTES

References are to the page and line of this edition;
there are 33 lines to the full page.

liver, brain, and heart: believed to be the seat of passion   P. 24 L. 11
and courage, intelligence and love.

Illyria: actually on the west coast of the Adriatic, but   P. 24 L. 20
Shakespeare uses it as the name of a picturesque and
imaginary kingdom.

bind himself ... to a strong mast: This detail Shakes-   P. 24 L. 30
peare may have taken from an incident in the Siege
of Ostend (July 1601): 'One man was very miracu-
lously saved who committed himself to the mercy of
God and the merciless seas upon a piece of a mast
rather than he would fall into the hands of his bloody
enemies. After he had so floated upon the waves of
the sea an hour or two he was taken up by another
ship which had spied the man thus driving on the
water.' [*Last Elizabethan Journal, p. 193.*]

Orion: the Folio reading. Arion the Singer is presum-   P. 25 L. 2
ably meant. He was captured by pirates who intend-
ed to kill him. He was allowed to sing for the last
time and then jumped into the sea where a dolphin,
fascinated by his song, carried him safe to land.

Orsino: Shakespeare here used the name of a distin-   P. 25 L. 14
guished foreign visitor, Virginio Orsino, Duke of
Brachiano, who visited Queen Elizabeth in January
1601.

for I can sing: As pointed out by Dr Dover Wilson, in   P. 26 L. 13
the play as first written, Viola was intended to be a
singer, but slight alterations were made (see note on
p. 51, l. 21) to transfer the songs to the Clown.

except before excepted: a legal phrase *exceptis excipien-*   P. 26 L. 29
dis.

tall: with the double meaning of 'high' and 'brave.'   P. 27 L. 10

P. 27 L. 21   *allay the gust:* water down the taste.

P. 27 L. 31   *parish-top:* a large whipping-top, used by the villagers on frosty days when it was too cold to work.

P. 27 L. 32   *Castiliano vulgo:* not satisfactorily explained, but the phrase means 'keep a straight face'.

P. 28 L. 6   *accost:* introduce yourself.

P. 28 L. 27   *buttery-bar:* the ledge on the half door leading to the pantry whereon pots are rested.

P. 28 L. 30   *It's dry:* a dry hand denoted lack of generosity and desire.

P. 29 L. 22   *cool my nature:* This is the Folio reading, usually altered to 'curl by nature'. Toby however is punning on 'air' and 'hair', 'art' and 'nature'. The modern stage convention is to give Sir Andrew blonde flaxen hair, but in Shakespeare's day it may have been red. If so the passage makes sense as it stands. The comparison with flax is not to the colour but to the texture and limpness of Andrew's locks, and for the sake of a dubious joke.

P. 30 L. 2   *Masques and Revels:* i.e. courtly entertainments.

P. 30 L. 8   *galliard ... caper ... back trick ... coranto ... jig ... sink-a-pace:* various kinds of steps in dancing; the galliard was quick and lively; a caper a jump in the air; coranto a quick running dance; a jig a fantastical dance; a sink-a-pace (cinque-pace) a dance of five steps.

P. 30 L. 15   *Mistress Mall's picture:* Mall or Moll is a common name for a prostitute. This particular lady may be Mistress Mall Newberry (see note on p. 62, l. 11) or one of her professional sisters.

P. 30 L. 23   *damn'd-colour'd:* The Folio reads 'dam'd'; editors emend to 'flame' or 'dun', 'damson', 'damask' etc. The colour of the damned is fire-red.

P. 30 L. 27   *Taurus? That's sides and heart.* The common penny almanack of the time (whence Andrew and many others fetched their knowledge of astrology) usually includes a figure of a naked man surrounded by the signs of the zodiac with lines pointing to the parts governed. Both knights are wrong: Taurus governs neck and throat, Sagittarius the thighs, and Aquarius the legs – as everyone in the audience knew.

civil bounds: restraints of good manners. P. 31 L. 25

grave aspect: sober countenance. P. 31 L. 32

colours: inevitable puns on 'collar' (halter), 'colour', and 'choler', which were pronounced alike. P. 32 L. 25

points: a pair of tagged laces which were tied to the doublet and so kept up the hose or breeches (*gaskins*). P. 33 L. 12

if Sir Toby ...: the first hint that Maria is setting her cap at Sir Toby. P. 33 L. 15

Enter Lady Olivia, with Malvolio: It was customary for younger sons and daughters of gentle, and sometimes noble birth, to take service in noblemen's houses as 'gentlemen serving-men' or 'gentlewomen'. Thus the steward of the northern estates of the Earl of Northumberland was his cousin Thomas Percy. Malvolio is not to be regarded as the butler, nor Maria as the lady's maid; both are of as good birth as Sir Toby. P. 33 L. 21

Quinapalus: Like Rabelais, the Clown is full of mock learning. P. 33 L. 25

Two faults ...: the Clown is in disgrace, and rattles out nonsense to cajole Olivia into good humour. P. 33 L. 31

Cucullus non facit monachum: 'the cowl does not make the monk.' P. 34 L. 10

Mouse of virtue: a term of familiar affection. P. 34 L. 18

barren rascal: By this rebuke Malvolio rouses the malice of the Clown and thereby brings about his own downfall. P. 35 L. 6

minister occasion: give him a lead. P. 35 L. 9

zanies: the zany is the Clown's assistant (or 'stooge') who tried to imitate his tricks. P. 35 L. 11

leasing: lying. Mercury was the god of thieves and rascals. P. 35 L. 19

pickle-herring: being very salt the pickled herring was indigestible, but encouraged a thirst. P. 36 L. 10

P. 36 L. 25   *the third degree of drink:* Nashe in *Piers Penniless* (edited by R. B. McKerrow, p. 207) declared that there were eight kinds of drunkenness: ape, lion, swine, sheep, maudlin, Martin (or puritanical), goat, and fox.

P. 37 L. 7   *sheriff's post:* a painted post set up outside a magistrate's house during his term of office so that he might be quickly found.

P. 37 L. 18   *standing water:* at the turn of the tide.

P. 38 L. 16   *from my commission:* not included in my instructions.

P. 38 L. 23   *allow'd ... hear you:* 'I allowed you to come in that I might observe one who was so impudent – not to listen to your tale.'

P. 38 L. 26   *time of moon:* lucky end of the month.

P. 38 L. 29   *good swabber:* Cesario answers 'hoist sail' with nautical metaphor; 'swabber' is one who swabs the decks;

P. 38 L. 29   *hull:* drift.

P. 38 L. 30   *some mollification for your giant:* Cesario apologises for digressing to answer Maria: 'I had to pacify your little lady.' Most editors redistribute these speeches, giving to Olivia 'Tell me your mind'.

P. 38 L. 32   *hideous matter ... fearful:* you must have some dreadful message to deliver if you need such an elaborate introduction.

P. 39 L. 15   *Where lies your text? In Orsino's bosom:* This 'hunting of the metaphor' is a good specimen of Elizabethan courtly wit at its best.

P. 39 L. 25   *such a one I was this present:* A puzzling phrase much emended by editors. The meaning is 'This is the picture I now present'.

P. 39 L. 28   *in grain:* the natural texture, not made up.

P. 40 L. 10   *Could be ... nonpareil of beauty:* 'only if you were an incomparable beauty could you be fit recompense for my master's love.'

P. 40 I. 19   *voices well divulg'd:* well spoken of by all.

P. 40 L. 24   *deadly life:* i.e. dying of love.

willow cabin: an arbour of willow – the tree especially P. 40 L. 28
favoured by unhappy lovers.

my soul: i.e. my true soul's mate. P. 40 L. 29

five-fold blazon: 'your speech etc. all proclaim that P. 41 L. 23
you are indeed a gentleman.' *Blazon:* the coat of
arms of a gentleman.

ourselves we do not owe: 'Fate, not ourselves, possesses P. 42 L. 10
us.'

Enter Antonio and Sebastian: In plays of mistaken per- P. 42 L. 14
sonality or misunderstanding it is Shakespeare's usual
custom to keep the audience informed and the characters ignorant. He prefers dramatic irony, both in
words and situation, to a surprise in the last Act.
Henceforward the main interest of the play is in the
reunion of brother and sister.

determinate voyage is mere extravagancy: my destina- P. 42 L. 24
tion is mere wandering. There is a touch of affecta-
tion in Sebastian's speech.

it charges me in manners: good manners demand. P. 42 L. 27

Enter Viola: To point the similarity of the twins, P. 44 L. 2
Viola enters as soon as Sebastian has gone.

She returns this ring: Note the Folio's effective punc- P. 44 L. 7
tuation of Malvolio's breathless speech.

desperate assurance: certainty that there is no hope. P. 44 L. 10

That sure methought: 'Sure' is not in the Folio but P. 44 L. 23
some such word is needed to fill out the metre.

proper-false: handsome but false. P. 45 L. 1

diluculo surgere: 'to rise early' – a tag from the Latin P. 45 L. 18
grammar which every schoolboy knew.

four elements: i.e. earth, air, fire, water, which were P. 45 L. 25
considered to be the ultimate forms of all matter.

the picture of we three: a picture of two fools, or asses, P. 46 L. 1
the beholder being the third.

catch: a rowdy song in which each singer catches up P. 46 L. 3
the song some words behind the others.

impeticos thy gratillity: 'pocket your tip.' The rest of P. 46 L. 11

the Clown's profundity is as yet not satisfactorily explained.

P. 47 L. 10   *dulcet in contagion:* sweetly catching.

P. 47 L. 12   *three souls out of one weaver:* Weavers were mostly Protestant refugees from the Netherlands, noted for their singing, especially of psalms.

P. 47 L. 12   *Catch:* The words of the Catch are *Hold thy peace,*

P. 47 L. 17   *thou knave.* See also note on p. 46, l. 3.

P. 47 L. 29   *My Lady's a Cataian:* Toby is now very drunk and his thoughts are connected loosely. In spite of much ingenuity no one has discovered why Olivia is a Cataian (Chinese) or what a Peg-a-Ramsey has to do with Malvolio.

P. 47 L. 31   *tillyvally:* an expression of disgust, of the 'hoity-toity' kind.

P. 47 L. 32   *There dwelt a man in Babylon:* The first verse of this godly ballad runs:
>   There dwelt a man in Babylon
>   Of reputation great by fame;
>   He took to wife a fair woman,
>   Susanna she was call'd by name:
>   A woman fair and virtuous;
>   Lady, lady:
>   Why should we not of her learn thus
>   To live godly?

P. 48 L. 4   *O the twelfth day of December:* this song is lost.

P. 48 L. 13   *Sneck up:* be hanged.

P. 48 L. 20   *Farewell, dear heart:* This ballad begins:
>   Farewell, dear love; since thou wilt needs be gone,
>   Mine eyes do shew, my life is almost done.
>   Nay I will never die, so long as I can spy
>   There be many mo, though that she do go,
>   There be many mo, I fear not:
>   Why then let her go, I care not.

P. 48 L. 27   *Shall I bid ...:* Toby and the Clown here indulge in an impromptu duet.

P. 48 L. 31   *cakes and ale:* 'good times.'

P. 49 L. 3   *chain:* his chain of office as steward.

common recreation : general laughing stock.   P. 49 L. 20

cons state without book : learns by heart courtly behav- P. 49 L. 30
iour.

Penthesilea : Queen of the Amazons, a large muscular P. 50 L. 29
lady, an ironical title for the little Maria.

foul way out : have wasted much money.   P. 51 L. 3

call me Cut : 'call me gelded.' The phrase is still used (I P. 51 L. 6
am informed) in Anglo-Irish country talk, and in the
proverb 'as cross as a cut cat'.

burn some sack : sack (a Spanish wine), Falstaff's fav- P. 51 L. 9
ourite drink. It was sometimes sweetened and drunk
warm.

recollected terms : artificial phrases.   P. 51 L. 18

He is not … sing it. This remark, after Cesario has P. 51 L. 21
been asked to sing, is one of the signs of adjustment
in the play (see note on p. 26, l. 13).

favour : lit. face. Viola in the safety of disguise takes P. 52 L. 8
up the word 'by your favour' which Orsino interprets
as 'by your leave'.

bent : tension (of a bow). 'A man who marries a P. 52 L. 24
woman older than himself cannot keep love taut.'

cypress : cypress usually means crêpe (as in p. 65, l. 20) P. 53 L. 9
but here may mean a coffin of cypress wood, or
strewn with branches of cypress.

My part of death : 'my participation in death,' i.e. dy- P. 53 L. 14
ing; but the exact meaning of Elizabethan lyrics is
never to be pressed too closely.

Give me now leave, to leave thee : exaggerated politeness P. 53 L. 29
for 'You may go'.

taffeta … opal … constancy : taffeta is shot silk whose P. 53 L. 31
colouring varies in different lights, as does the colour
of an opal – like Orsino's wavering affections.

sat like Patience : i.e. a statue of Patience.   P. 55 L. 10

bear-baiting : regarded as rather a low amusement, P. 55 L. 31
and much disliked by Puritans.

metal of India : The Folio reads 'nettle'. The 'metal of P. 56 L. 0
India' is gold.

P. 56 L. 11   *contemplative idiot:* pompous ass.

P. 56 L. 12   *trout ... with tickling:* A poacher's method of catching trout with the hands.

P. 56 L. 24   *jets under his advanc'd plumes:* struts with his tail feathers up.

P. 56 L. 31   *the Lady of the Strachy, married the yeoman of the wardrobe:* No one has yet discovered who the Lady was. Such a match was however not unknown. The Earl of Essex's mother took as her second husband the Earl of Leicester, and on his death married Christopher Blount, his master of horse.

P. 56 L. 33   *Jezebel:* Sir Andrew's scriptural knowledge is weak, but at least he knows that Jezebel was a shameless person.

P. 57 L. 12   *demure travel of regard:* looking over them with a dignified glance.

P. 57 L. 25   *austere regard of control:* stern look of authority.

P. 58 L. 8   *spirit of humours:* i.e. of mockery.

P. 58 L. 11   *Her C's, her U's and her T's ... great P's:* One modern critic notes: 'Readers and actors have been repeating Sir Andrew's question for 300 years without finding an answer, except that Shakespeare's "regal indolence" did not trouble to make the letters correspond with anything in the superscription which Malvolio reads out. (cf. Robert Bridges, *Collected Essays,* i. 27-28). But if it is carelessness why does Sir Andrew underline it in this way? His question surely makes it certain that the letters possessed some point for Shakespeare's audience which now escapes us.' A knowledge of the vulgar tongue is desirable in editing Shakespeare, for any sailor could explain the joke – such as it is.

P. 58 L. 16   *her Lucrece:* seal engraved with the head of Lucrece.

P. 58 L. 28   *fustian:* literally, coarse cloth, so 'bombastic'.

P. 58 L. 33   *staniel:* kestrel, an emendation for the Folio 'stallion'.

P. 59 L. 3   *formal capacity:* normal intelligence.

P. 59 L. 8   *cry upon't ... fox:* 'he will get excited about it and pick up his scent however rank.'

no consonancy ... probation: there is no consistency in what follows; it fails upon testing. P. 59 L. 13

slough, and appear fresh: i.e. like a snake that has shed its old skin. P. 59 L. 31

trick of singularity: behave in a peculiar way. P. 59 L. 33

yellow stockings ... cross garter'd: Yellow included all shades from orange to lemon. In the Lancaster possession (1597) one of the girls was possessed with a 'spirit of pride' which caused her to long for 'hose of orange colour, this is in request'. [*Second Elizabethan Journal*, p. 178.] P. 60 L. 1

'Cross garters, which were placed around the leg below the knee, twisted crosswise in the back, brought forward above the knee, and tied in a bow on the side, were fashionable from the sixties, and though still used by gentlemen after 1600, according to *The Woman Hunter*, their decline began with the introduction of knee-length breeches, and by 1600 they were worn chiefly by old men, Puritans, pedants, footmen, and rustic bridegrooms'. [M. C. Linthicum. *Costume in Elizabethan Drama*, pp. 264, 47.]

Jove: for 'God', to avoid offending against the Statute of 1606 which forbade the name of God to be used on the stage. P. 60 L. 19

Sophy: the Shah of Persia. In 1597 Sir Anthony Shirley (a notable swashbuckler) went on a mission to the Shah and was very kindly received. From Kasvin the party proceeded to Russia, whence news of them reached England in 1600. In the autumn of 1601 an account of their journeyings and troubles was published, which Shakespeare seems to have read. Shirley's adventures were much talked of. P. 60 L. 20

yellow ... colour she abhors: though Malvolio himself thought she adored it. P. 61 L. 15

my sister had had no name: There is obviously some topical jest in this talk of 'sister' and 'wanton', probably referring to the notorious case of Moll Newberry *alias* Fowler. This woman turned prostitute, P. 62 L. 11

and to get rid of her husband, framed a false accusation of high treason against him. She and her brother were brought before the Court of the Star Chamber in June 1600. She was sentenced to whipping and perpetual imprisonment, and her brother for acting as bawd to his own sister was fined £100. [*Last Elizabethan Journal*, pp. 89, 90.]

P. 62 L. 15   *words ... bonds disgrac'd them:* The right reading is probably 'bawds'; bawd (spelt 'baud') and bond are sometimes confused, as in *Hamlet* I. 3, 129:

    'But mere implorators of unholy suits,
    Breathing like sanctified and pious bonds,
    The better to beguile';
Usually emended to 'pious bawds'.

P. 63 L. 3   *pass upon me:* make a thrust at.

P. 63 L. 18   *welkin ... element:* Both words mean 'sky' or 'climate'. 'Element' was mocked at in Dekker's *Satiromastix* (Autumn 1601), a play in which he answered and attacked Ben Jonson's *Poetaster*. Fashions in words at this time were variable and nice. 'Element' is still overworn in critical jargon; no text book can avoid the 'supernatural *element*', 'the fairy *element*' and the like.

P. 63 l. 21   *This fellow is wise enough to play the fool:* In this speech Shakespeare goes out of his way to compliment Robert Armin, the new clown of the Chamberlain's Company, who had succeeded the famous Will Kemp. 'One of Armin's particular accomplishments was to compose extempore verses. He would ask the audience to suggest a subject and thereupon would produce a poem out of his head. ... Armin had published a collection of these trifles in 1600 during the lean weeks caused by the Council's inhibition on playing, and one of the pieces was on the Fool:

    True it is, he plays the fool indeed;
    But in the play, he plays it as he must;
    Yet when the play is ended, then this speech
    Is better than the pleasure of thy trust:
      For he shall have what thou that time hast spent,

Playing the fool thy folly to content,

He plays the wise man then, and not the fool,
That wisely for his living so can do:
So doth the carpenter with his sharp tool,
Cut his own finger oft, yet lives by't too.
    He is a fool to cut his limb, say I,
    But not so with his tool to love thereby …

Armin ended this extempore effort with a quip
which ran:

A merry man is often thought unwise,
Yet mirth in modesty's lov'd of the wise:
Then say, should he for a fool go?
When he's more fool that accounts him so?
Many men descant on another's wit,
When they have less themselves in doing it'.

                    (*Shakespeare at Work*, pp. 295–296)

Shakespeare, by thus incorporating Armin's verses.
pointed the contrast between the new clown and the
old low comedian. Kemp at the time was acting with
a rival company at the Rose Theatre, hardly a stone's
throw from the Globe.

And like the haggard, check at every feather: 'And like a P. 63 L. 25
wild hawk swoop on every small bird.'   Some edi-
tors prefer to read '*Not* like'.

music from the spheres: According to Pythagoras, P. 65 L. 8
whose astronomical notions were still generally accepted, the seven planets in their motion each emitted
a different musical note, all together producing a
heavenly harmony.

baited … unmuzzl'd: like the bear torn by the hounds P. 65 L. 18
in bear baiting.

westward-ho: the Thames watermen's cry. P. 66 L. 3

Do not … better: 'Do not argue to yourself that, be- P. 66 L. 21
cause I (the woman) am the wooer, you have no
cause to return my love; but rather answer that argument with this – it is good to ask for a woman's love,
but better to receive it without asking.'

dear venom: 'dear spitfire.'   P. 67 L. 4

P. 67 L. 17 *grand-jurymen:* 'Messrs. Judgment and Reason have been of the highest respectability since Noah.' The grand-jury was composed of the most responsible citizens. 'You are grand-jurors, are ye?' cries Falstaff to the wealthy merchants as he robs them, 'we'll jure ye, i' faith.'

P. 67 L. 25 *double gilt:* The best gilt plate was dipped twice. Fabian and Toby amuse themselves by puzzling Andrew with this highly metaphorized talk.

P. 68 L. 1 *Brownist:* one of the extreme Puritan sects; or as a modern Sir Andrew might say, 'a Communist.'

P. 68 L. 14 *if thou thou'st him some thrice:* To call a man 'thou' was insulting. Thus in a quarrel between a Mr. Edward Darcy and Sir George Barnes in 1593, Mr. Darcy 'in a very unseemly and unreverent manner "*thou'd*" Sir George Barnes. ... Not content withal he suddenly strake Sir George with his fist on the face.' [*An Elizabethan Journal*, p. 216]. Similarly Coke the Attorney General 'thou'd' Raleigh at his trial. The passage is *not* a reference to this event which occurred more than a year after *Twelfth Night* was acted.

P. 68 L. 17 *bed of Ware:* This famous relic, which on occasion has held twelve couples, is now in the Victoria and Albert Museum.

P. 68 L. 32 *blood in his liver:* a bloodless liver denotes a coward.

P. 69 L. 4 *youngest wren of nine:* One in a brood or litter is often smaller than the rest. So Maria is likened to the littlest of a brood of wrens.

P. 69 L. 12 *school i' th' church:* churches often served as schoolrooms.

P. 69 L. 16 *new map with the augmentation of the Indies:* 'A peculiar interest attaches to this map, not because it includes the Indies – every map of the world published during the sixteenth century did that – but because we know its date (1600) and its authors. Edward Wright drew it, Richard Hakluyt and John Davies helped in its preparation; and it was the first English map that was drawn on what are called Mercator's principles of projection, – principles which were discovered not by Mercator, it would appear, but by Edward Wright ... It appealed, however, to Shakespeare because its rhumb-lines illustrated Malvolio's smiles.' [*Shakespeare's England*, i, 174.] Rhumb-lines are numerous lines radiating from various points to indicate the course of ships sailing from that point in various directions.

the Elephant: Here Shakespeare apparently gives a free advertisement to the inn which is now called the 'Elephant and Castle'. P. 71 L. 1

possess'd: i.e. with an evil spirit. P. 71 L. 23

true sonnet is: Please one, and please all: 'Sonnet' at this time is used generally of songs as well as poems in the sonnet form. Malvolio's sonnet begins: P. 72 L. 7

> The crow sits upon the wall
> Please one and please all: –

not at all the kind of song that Malvolio might be expected to sing.

Roman hand: The Italian style of writing (from which modern handwriting and *italic* type derives) was coming into fashion among aristocratic writers, and superseding the old 'court' or 'secretary' hand. P. 72 L. 12

Legion himself possess'd him: Toby and the rest here pretend that the steward is possessed by evil spirits like the victims whom Darrell exorcised, and treat him accordingly. [See Introduction, p. 18.] For Malvolio to resent the suggestion that he should say his prayers was a sign that he had been bewitched. Suspected witches were made to repeat the Lord's Prayer; if they faltered it was a sure sign of guilt. P. 74 L. 5

Carry his water: diagnosis of diseases by inspection of the urine was commonly practised as well by qualified doctors as by quacks. P. 74 L. 22

cherry-pit: a childish game of throwing cherry stones into a hole. P. 75 L. 3

collier: because Satan is black and familiar with coals. P. 75 L. 4

device to the bar: bring our plot to open judgment. P. 75 L. 27

thou liest in thy throat: To 'give a man the lie' was a mortal insult; to say 'he lied in his throat' was worse. P. 76 L. 10

A man who refused to fight on being given the lie branded himself a coward.

P. 76 L. 17   *windy side of the Law*: i.e. on the right side, to the windward.

P. 77 L. 16   *cockatrices*: a fabulous beast, being a snake hatched out of a cock's egg, able to slay with its glance.

P. 78 L. 26   *unhatch'd ... carpet consideration*: Sir Andrew is a 'carpet knight', who has knelt for his accolade on a carpet not a battle field. *Unhatched*: unhacked in fight.

P. 79 L. 19   *mortal arbitrement*: a fight to the death.

P. 79 L. 29   *Sir Priest*: Those who had taken their bachelor's degree were termed 'Dominus'; in lists at Cambridge the B.A.'s are still noted as 'Ds'. Hence as most priests were graduates they were called 'Sir.'

P. 80 L. 1   *firago*: for virago, a masculine woman – which Cesario most certainly was not.

P. 80 L. 5   *fencer to the Sophy*: See note on p. 60, l. 29.

P. 80 L. 19   *as horribly conceited*: has as horrible ideas of.

P. 80 L. 31   *Duello*: the laws of duelling, which amongst gentlemen were as punctiliously regarded as a ruling by the M.C.C.

P. 83 L. 3   *trunks o'er flourish'd*: the chests used for storing clothes, elaborately carved.

P. 83 L. 14   *He nam'd Sebastian*: Viola at once realizes that the mistake can only have been made because Sebastian, after all, is alive.

P. 84 L. 15   *Cockney*: (originally 'a cock's egg') a spoilt child.

P. 84 L. 19   *foolish Greek*: foolish wag.

P. 85 L. 11   *young soldier ... well flesh'd*: Some critics take this as referring to Sir Andrew. Toby however tells Sebastian that like a young soldier in his first action he has fleshed (i.e. blooded) his sword well – has shown sufficient courage. Since they mistake Sebastian for Viola it follows that he looks very young.

P. 85 L. 17   *malapert*: impudent. Toby at first was willing to treat Sebastian as a boy but now he loses his temper.

P. 86 L. 5   *Lethe*: the River of Forgetfulness in the underworld.

Curate: i.e. the vicar.   P. 86 L. 15

good housekeeper: one who keeps a good table.   P. 86 L. 22

competitors: conspirators.   P. 86 L. 24

King Gorboduc: one of the legendary kings invented   P. 86 L. 29
by early chroniclers to fill the gaps in English History
before records began.

peace in this prison: Here the Clown affects the par-   P. 87 L. 2
sonical voice.

barricadoes: a hybrid, military Spanish form, as were   P. 87 L. 21
most military terms at this time. The Clown is talk-
ing deliberate nonsense to baffle Malvolio.

clearstores: clerestories, the upper line of windows in   P. 87 L. 22
a church or hall.

Egyptians in their fog: 'And the Lord said unto Moses,   P. 87 L. 29
Stretch out thine hand toward heaven, that there
may be darkness in all the land of Egypt, even darkness which may be felt ... and there was a thick darkness in all the land of Egypt three days, they saw not
one another, neither rose any from his place for three
days.' [*Exodus* x. 21.]

constant question: i.e. a question requiring intelligent   P. 87 L. 33
answers.

opinion of Pythagoras: i.e. that human souls may trans-   P. 88 L. 1
migrate into animals.

Fare thee well: The Clown parodies the visitation by   P. 88 L. 8
the minister of a man possessed.

I am for all waters: the origin of the phrase is doubt-   P. 88 L. 14
ful; it means 'I can make myself at home anywhere'.

Hey Robin, jolly Robin. The song begins: P. 88 L. 24
> A Robyn,
>   Jolly Robyn,
> Tell me how thy leman doth,
>   And thou shalt know of mine.
> 'My lady is unkind perde.'
> Alack! why is she so?
> 'She loveth an other better than me;
> And yet she will say no.'

P. 89 L. 5   *five wits:* i.e. common wit, imagination, fantasy, estimation, memory.

P. 89 L. 15   *thy vain bibble babble:* In the Lancaster possession case, when the ministers arrived and called for a Bible, the children laughed and said, 'Reach them the bibble-babble, bibble-babble.' See note on p. 60, l. 1.

P. 89 L. 18   *God buy you:* The usual Folio spelling of the phrase, meaning 'God be with you'.

P. 90 L. 7   *Vice:* a character which often occurred in the old Morality Plays, where it thumped the Devil with a wooden sword, and tried to pare his nails.

P. 91 L. 12   *Plight me the full assurance:* Olivia demands not marriage, but formal betrothal before witnesses, which at this time was legally binding.

P 91 L. 30   *in recompense desire my dog again:* A well-known story given in Manningham's diary: 'Mr. Francis Curle told me how one Dr. Bullein, the Queen's kinsman, had a dog which he doted on, so much that the Queen understanding of it requested he would grant her one desire, and he should have whatsoever he would ask. She demanded his dog; he gave it, and 'Now, Madam,' quoth he, 'you promised to give me my desire.' 'I will,' quoth she. 'Then I pray you give me my dog again.'

P. 92 L. 13   *conclusions to be as kisses:* i.e. as a kiss stops all lovers' arguments.

P. 92 L. 30   *Saint Bennet:* Saint Benedict, a famous London church.

P. 93 L. 15   *scathful grapple ... on him:* 'He made so damaging an attack on the finest vessel of our fleet that in spite of our anger and loss we were forced to applaud his courage.'

P. 94 L. 22   *three months:* On the stage these words give the general impression of the passage of time: when the play is carefully read it appears that the whole action has only taken three days. Such 'time-problems' are common in Shakespeare's plays.

Egyptian thief : The story is that Thyamis, an Egypti- P. 95 L. 17
an brigand, captured Chariclea and shut her in a cave.
Being attacked and defeated by other robbers, he
rushed into the cave to slay her rather than that she
should fall into other hands.

husband, stay : The betrothal had made the supposed P. 96 L. 11
Cesario Olivia's legal husband.

strangle thy propriety : choke your proper self, i.e. be- P. 96 L. 17
have like a coward.

grizzle on thy case : when Time has sown grey hairs. P. 97 L. 4
case : outside.

Or will ... overthrow : 'unless your trickery leads you P. 97 L. 5
to an earlier death.'

passy measures pavin : The Folio reads 'panyn' (mis- P. 98 L. 8
print for 'pauyn'). The clown's 'set at eight' stirs in
Toby the fuddled recollection that there were eight
'strains' in a *passa measures pavan* or a slow, stately
dance.

thin-fac'd knave : Shakespeare several times calls atten- P. 98 L. 15
tion to the thinness of one of his characters. Prince
Hal is a 'tailor's yard'; Shadow (in *II Henry IV*) a
'half-faced fellow'; the beadle in the same play 'a
starved bloodhound'; whilst Slender is a 'latten
bilbo' and has a 'little wee face'. Shakespeare wrote
his plays to suit the individuals of his company and
he made use of these physical pecularities.

A natural perspective : A perspective is a picture which P. 98 L. 27
from in front has one appearance, but looked at from
the side is quite different. There is a 'perspective portrait' of Edward VI in the National Portrait Gallery.

Do I stand there? : This is the final shock to Sebastian. P. 99 L. 4
He has suddenly fallen into a lunatics' world where
he is greeted familiarly by a fool, assaulted by strang-
ers, rescued and entertained by a beautiful lady, and
finally precipitately betrothed. Now apparently he
sees himself standing opposite himself.

deity ... every where : I am not a god to be in two P. 99 L. 5
places at once.

P. 99 L. 16   *that dimension grossly clad:* i.e. enclosed in that bodily form.

P. 100 L. 6   *bias:* natural inclination, as of the bowl which is weighted to take a curved course.

P. 100 L. 17   *orbed continent, the fire:* i.e. the sun.

P. 100 L. 29   *extracting:* that drew out all other thoughts.

P. 101 L. 9   *allow Vox:* i.e. let me read in the tones appropriate to a madman.

P. 101 L. 20   *I leave ... my injury:* i.e. I do not write in the formal phrase proper to your steward.

P. 102 L. 15   *Write from it:* i.e. you cannot deny that it is your handwriting or style.

P. 104 L. 7   *Exeunt all but the Clown:* The Clown is a most important person in the play: he is the link between the different sets of characters. At the beginning of the play he was in danger of being turned away: now he most certainly has lost his job. As the others leave him he sings this little song which sums up the whole of his experience: it gives that note of questioning which often ends one of Shakespeare's comedies. It was common for the Clown to have the stage to himself at the end of the play when he danced and sang his jig. This song is part jig.

P. 104 L. 21   *But when ... unto my beds:* A difficult stanza, variously emended. It means, probably, 'at the end of my life.'

GLOSSARY

admire : be astonished
affection'd : affected
approbation : approval

babbling gossip : echo
baffled : disgraced
balked : blocked neglected
barful : full of impediments
bawbling : trifling
bawcock : fine fellow (*beau coq*)
beagle : little hound
beshrew : ill luck take
bespeak : order
blent : blended
bones : bone bobbins
botched : patched.
botcher : jobbing tailor
brabble : brawl
branch'd : embroidered with a pattern of leaves and branches
breach : breaking
breast : voice
brock : badger
bum-bailey : an officer who arrests for debt

Canary : dry wine from the Canarie
Candy : Crete

cantons : canzons, songs
car : chariot
champain : open country
chantry : chapel
character : (a) handwriting. (b) outward appearance
cheveril : soft leather
churchman : clergyman
civil : sober
clodpole : lit. with a head like a clod
cloistress : nun
coffer : chest, i.e. purse
comedian : stage player
competitors : conspirators
comptible : susceptible
con : learn by heart
consanguineous : related by blood
conster : construe, translate
construction : interpretation
contemn'd : despised
County : Count
cousin : kinsman
coystrill : knave
cozier : cobbler
credit : report
crowner : coroner
Cubiculo : bedchamber
curst : shrewish, tart

cypress: (a) a coffin of cypress wood. (b) A semi-transparent material

damask: pink and white – the colour of damask roses
daws: jackdaws
daybed: couch
degree: rank
delivered: discovered
despite: spite
dissemble: disguise
distemper: disorder
distraction: madness
driving: driven before the wind

element: sky
estimable: admirable, admiring
extent: attack

fadge: turn out
fall: cadence
fancy: love
fantastical: full of fantasies
fat: sickly
fault: check in following the scent
favour: face
fee'd post: hired messenger
feelingly: exactly
formal capacity: normal understanding
fraught: freight
free: innocent
fulsome: nauseous

geck: dupe
genius: guardian angel
glass: reflection
grize: step
gull: fool
gust: relish

halting: limping
hie: hasten
hob, nob: hit or miss
humour: whim
humour of state: manners affected by a statesman
hyperbolical: extravagant

importance: importunity
incardinate: incarnate

jade me: play a dirty trick on me
iealousy: anxiety

kickchawses: kickshaws, fancy trifles
kindness: natural love

lapsed: caught
leman: love
lenten: lean
lethargy: insensibility
lets: hinders
lim'd: caught with bird lime
list: limit, objective
love-broker: match maker

mellifluous: honey sweet
minion: darling
misprision: mistake
mortal motion: deadly action
motley: the fool's party-colour-
ed uniform

natural: silly
nayword: by-word
nonpareil: without an equal
numbers: poetic metre
nuntio: messenger

'Ods bodykins: by God's little
body
opposite: opponent
othergates: otherwise
overture: declaration
owe: possess

parts: wealth
perdy: by God
perpend: attend
pia mater: the thin skin cover-
ing the brain
pitch: height
point-devise: meticulously
pranks: decks out
pregnant: apt, receptive
prerogative: privilege
presently: immediately
prevented: forestalled
proof: experience, example
propertied: treated like a piece
of furniture

propriety: natural quality

quirk: peculiar behaviour
quits: discharges

receiving: apprehension
reliques: antiquities
renegado: a Christian who has
renounced his faith
round: 'straight'
rudesby: ruffian

sage saws: wise sayings
screws: wrenches
season: keep untainted, as meat
in brine
set: closed
sheep-biter: dog that worries
the sheep, cur
shent: rebuked
silly sooth: simple truth
skipping: frivolous
'Slid: by God's eyelid
Sowter: botcher, bungler, the
name of a hound
squash: unripe pea-pod
still: always
stone-bow: cross-bow shooting
stones or bullets
stout: haughty
substractors: detractors
syllogism: logical argument

tabor: small drum carried by
fools

tall: brave

Tartar: Hell

taxation: claim for

testril: coin worth sixpence

thriftless: useless

trappings: ornaments

tray-trip: a dice game at which the winning throw was three (*trey*)

tuck: rapier

unchary: without stinting

uncivil: disorderly

undertaker: meddler

unprizable: valueless

upshot: conclusion

validity: value

vent: utter

viol-de-gamboys: base-viol, held between the legs

vouchsaf'd: condescending

vulgar proof: common example

wain ropes: cart ropes

weeds: garments

welkin: sky

well-favour'd: with a handsome face

whiles: until

PENGUIN POPULAR CLASSICS

Published or forthcoming

Aesop	Aesop's Fables
Hans Andersen	Fairy Tales
Louisa May Alcott	Good Wives
	Little Women
Eleanor Atkinson	Greyfriars Bobby
Jane Austen	Emma
	Mansfield Park
	Northanger Abbey
	Persuasion
	Pride and Prejudice
	Sense and Sensibility
R. M. Ballantyne	The Coral Island
J. M. Barrie	Peter Pan
R. D. Blackmore	Lorna Doone
Anne Brontë	Agnes Grey
	The Tenant of Wildfell Hall
Charlotte Brontë	Jane Eyre
	The Professor
	Shirley
	Villette
Emily Brontë	Wuthering Heights
John Buchan	The Thirty-Nine Steps
Frances Hodgson Burnett	A Little Princess
	The Secret Garden
Samuel Butler	The Way of All Flesh
Lewis Carroll	Alice's Adventures in Wonderland
	Through the Looking Glass
Geoffrey Chaucer	The Canterbury Tales
G. K. Chesterton	Father Brown Stories
Erskine Childers	The Riddle of the Sands
John Cleland	Fanny Hill
Wilkie Collins	The Moonstone
	The Woman in White
Sir Arthur Conan Doyle	The Adventures of Sherlock Holmes
	The Hound of the Baskervilles
	A Study in Scarlet